S0-BCI-676

KILLERS

No Faith in Cats

NICOLE M. TAYLOR

E

EPIC
Press

No Faith in Cats
Killers

Written by Nicole M. Taylor

Copyright © 2017 by Abdo Consulting Group, Inc.

Published by EPIC Press™
PO Box 398166
Minneapolis, MN 55439

Printed in the United States of America.

Cover design by Christina Doffing
Images for cover art obtained from iStockPhoto.com
Edited by Jennifer Skogen

LIBRARY OF CONGRESS CATALOGING-IN-PUBLICATION DATA

Names: Taylor, Nicole M., author.
Title: No faith in cats / by Nicole M. Taylor.
Description: Minneapolis, MN : EPIC Press, 2017. | Series: Killers
Summary: A superficially charming young trophy wife hides a dark secret: she is deliberately,
    sometimes compulsively, poisoning the people around her. A suspicious ER nurse with a
    dark side of his own vows to make her pay for her crimes.
Identifiers: LCCN 2016946205 | ISBN 9781680764871 (lib. bdg.) |
    ISBN 9781680765434 (ebook)
Subjects: LCSH: Women murderers—Fiction. | Murder—Investigation—Fiction. | Poisons—
    Fiction. | Mystery and detective stories—Fiction. | Young adult fiction.
Classification: DDC [Fic]—dc23
LC record available at http://lccn.loc.gov/2016946205

EPIC
Press

EPICPRESS.COM

For Nicki B.,
plant lady and stalwart friend.
Much love, my dear.

Lydia Sherman is plagued with rats
Lydia has no faith in cats.
So Lydia buys some arsenic,
And then her husband gets sick;
And then her husband, he does die,
And Lydia's neighbors wonder why?
    —Folk rhyme, traditional

1

White Snakeroot

A wild plant containing a toxin called tremetol. Poisoning usually occurs indirectly, after a person drinks milk or eats meat from cattle that have grazed upon the plant.

If you want to get persnickety about it, Benji's birthday was on Wednesday—but who goes to a party on a Wednesday? No, Saturday worked better for everything.

It's a lot to keep track of, planning a party. Everyone pretends it's soooo easy, like any idiot could do it, but there's really a lot of moving parts. For example: Sundays—especially Sunday evenings—are, on average, the busiest times for an emergency room. Saturdays are calm in comparison.

That meant Benji would be sure to get the attention he deserved.

I'd even started to research which hospital he was likely to be routed to, based on average patient load and proximity and there were really only a couple of options. Rich people only went to hospitals of a certain caliber, and just as Benji would never have stayed in a Motel 6, he wasn't going to be sent to the overstuffed county hospital either.

I initially forgot these things because I wasn't a rich person—I was just married to one. Soon, though, I'd have money all my own and I'd have to know all of this like an instinct.

Benji and I were married for almost exactly two years, but I knew everything I needed to know about him long before we walked down the aisle (or, stood in line at the county courthouse). I'd been with my first husband when I met Benji and his sister Clara at an art auction. Jakob—my first husband's name was Jakob—already knew them, of course. The Fraye siblings, the last heirs. Both of them had the good kind of plastic surgery, the kind that Jakob had to tell me about because I couldn't tell just from looking at them.

Benji was rich, but not the sort of rich where you had a company or made up some kind of crazy invention. He was rich because his father had been rich, who had been rich because *his* father had been rich. And all this meant that he wasn't nearly as rich as he might have been, if he'd been born a generation earlier.

Jakob, who *was* the sort of rich that comes from founding a company, explained to me how that was the way money always goes. "That's why," he said, "we'll teach our kids better. They'll know the value of a dollar."

As if I was ever going to push his kids out my down-below!

I hadn't been meaning to jump ship when I met Benji, but I have always been impatient. My mother used to chide me for it all the time, and I think it is my great flaw. I got ahead of myself, got a little bit careless and . . . well, it all worked out in the end, so I can't really say that I regret it, but I do think about it from time to time, about how it might have gone differently.

With Benji, though, I was focused and in control. I'd made a plan and I was sticking to it! I think my mama would've been proud of me; she would've said that I was growing and coming into my own as a woman.

It's incredible, how often she comes into my mind. I think about her every day, wondering what she would've done in my situation, wondering how she would've felt about me, wondering if she'd like me as I am now. I suppose a girl never really leaves her raising behind, no matter how far she goes.

·   ·   ·

I remember the first time I saw an apartment building. It was on TV and I was eight years old. It looked about as real to me as Cinderella's castle.

(Later, I found out that Cinderella's castle really does exist, sort of, but no one really lives there. Lots of real people live in apartments.)

And now look at me!

My home (well, Benji's home) was a four-teen-room mansion with a long, tapering pool that overlooked the whole city. I liked to go out there at night, after Benji had already gone to sleep. I never learned how to swim, so I'd cling real tight to the far end of the pool, concrete pricking at my bare arms. I'd look down and see the electric-lit hills melting into one another like cats sleeping all in a huddle. I liked to imagine that someone could be living down there, maybe in some shitty little apartment next to a Mexican grocery store or a gas station and that they were looking up at our home, a white protrusion impossibly far above them. Maybe they even tried to picture someone like me in their minds, someone beautiful and remote.

I have always been beautiful. I was the kind of kid people would have stopped on the street to compliment, except that we almost never went out in public. Still, I could see just from looking at my siblings and my parents that I was something special.

Mommie had told me as much, too. She'd warned me that the way I looked was not a gift from God but challenge from the Devil.

"The enemy is always waiting, just waiting for us to stumble," she'd said. "He made you beautiful so it would be easier for you to fall into the sin of pride. You have to guard your heart against it."

Mommie had told me it was my burden, one of many, and it wasn't until long after she was dead that I realized beauty is also a tool.

Everyone likes beautiful people, especially rich people. You can tell, because it's the first thing anyone tries to buy when they get a little bit of money.

That was how I got Benji! It was true what Jakob said about Benji's family fortune steadily draining away over the years, but while it may not have made Benji particularly frugal, it did make him gun-shy in certain ways. He didn't have no ex-wives, no kids (at least not any that were willing to prove it in court). Benji meant to keep that fraction of a fortune he had left, and he lorded over it like a dragon on his treasure-pile. But he was getting old—and nobody can escape *that*. Old people start thinking more and more about what the end of their lives are going to look like, who's gonna be there to hold their hands or whatever. Benji was just like anyone else; he wanted someone nice to look at, who would say kind things to him while he died.

Benji liked me right away. He shook my hand too long and held me too high up on my wrist. He helped me put my coat on when we were leaving and let his hand trail down my back. Every time he looked at me, it was like a proposition.

It was clear that I was there with Jakob. It was even clear that I was married to Jakob, but Benji didn't seem bothered by any of that. He had an aura of patience about him that made him seem even older than he was. Jakob had taken a rare Picasso sculpture home from the auction and Benji probably figured that, if he waited long enough, he could buy that out from under Jakob too. Considering the way it all went down, I bet you anything Benji thought he'd actually won. He never realized, though, that he wasn't playing against Jakob. He was playing against *me*.

Jakob and I had laughed at him on the plane back home to Los Angeles—at what an old perv he was—and that was when Jakob told me all about the Frayes—specifically Benji's father, who had lost the lion's share of their money on shaky real estate investments and a succession of bad marriages (including the one to Benji's mother).

I think Jakob had meant it to be a story about how unearned Benji's air of unruffled confidence was, but I'd filed it all away in my brain. I'd thought that, when the time came and I had gotten everything I needed from Jakob, I would move on to a softer target like Benji. After Jakob, I hadn't wanted to bother with another young and hungry entrepreneur.

I'd meant to stay married to Jakob for a few years at least. He was supposed to be my launch-pad husband, vaulting me into the world of the truly wealthy. Instead, we only made it eight months. It was my fault, I suppose, but I never really meant for it to happen like it did.

I only started dosing him because, otherwise, he would have been gone all the time. He was always flying off somewhere—to Dubai or London or Russia—and he barely had any time for me. I was lucky if I got a kiss on the cheek and a quickie in the hotel lobby bathroom before he went back out again. All I wanted was to slow him down just a little bit and make him smell the roses. Or smell me, at least.

I didn't give him a giant dose or anything. In fact, it was probably even smaller than I would usually do because it was the first time. He should have just felt a little sick—nauseous and dizzy and tired, like a flu bug. I would have locked him up in the hotel with me and told him sternly that he had to feel better before he could travel again. I would have ordered homemade chicken noodle soup and freshly squeezed orange juice from room service. I would have helped him to the bathroom when he had to puke and I would have rubbed his back while he retched. Afterward, I would've lain in bed with him and put a cool cloth on his forehead and we would've always remembered that time, that good time, when I'd taken perfect care of him.

He must have been allergic or something. How could I have known about something like that? *He* probably didn't even know about it. Wild crows-hood isn't the kind of thing that people come across in their everyday lives.

I'd known something was wrong when he wouldn't stop puking, not even after the blood vessels in his eyes burst and flooded them with red. Soon there was blood in the vomit too, and he couldn't hold his bowels. I set him up in the bath-tub so he wouldn't mess on the bathroom floor.

He kept reaching out for me, grabbing at the edge of my shirt with weak fingers. That was some-thing I liked to see, even though it meant he was in a bad way. I wanted him to want me, after all.

The doctors were baffled by his condition. Their best theory was that he had contracted some sort of exotic disease, probably from all of his darting back and forth across the world. I made it clear, though, that I didn't want any extraordinary measures—no special research or autopsies—and once it became clear that he was not contagious, they gave me my way.

Most of the time, people do. No one wants to do more work and absolutely no one wants to tell a grieving young widow that she can't bury her hus-band promptly.

But that was a flub—I am a big enough person to admit that. I didn't get anything out of it, either. Jakob and I had been married less than a year, my name wasn't on anything that mattered, and I was nowhere near the end of my prenup.

After Jakob, I was afraid. I'm not sure exactly what would have happened if I hadn't met Benji again at the funeral. I didn't have any settlements; we hadn't even set up any kind of life insurance provision for me. I had the things Jakob had given me, and the hotel room was paid up through the end of the month, but after that . . .

Well, I *did* meet Benji, so there's no real point in dwelling on what might have been. Four days after the funeral, I was in the guest house at his San Diego home. Three days after that, I was in the main house with him. Two weeks later, I was well on my way to becoming Mrs. Benji Fraye.

This time, I knew I had to be even more patient, even more careful. I'd liked Jakob—maybe that was the problem. He was only forty-two and good looking. I'd liked it when he touched me and looked at me and gave me things. I'd wanted him around so I felt less alone. It was that wanting that led me to try too much too fast and ruin everything for myself.

Fortunately, Benji wasn't very likable at all.

He was halfway to deaf in one ear and he had all-gray hair. He was incredibly boring and often got distracted, just looking at nothing in particular, and barely even noticing when I was in the room. The only thing I liked about him was the way his hands would tremble a little bit when he touched me. He had been rich all his life and he had been with all sorts of beautiful women in his time, but when I took off my clothes, he shook like a teenage boy seeing his first pair of boobs.

This time, I got everything in order right from the start. First, I tested him before we even officially got married, giving him just the tiniest pinch of dried wild crowshood, and when I noticed no seriously ill effects, I worked up from there until I'd given him a very bad weekend. I, of course, stayed with him all that time, coddling him like a huge, gray baby.

That part was okay. Benji was quiet when he was sick and he didn't want to talk at me for hours and hours; all he wanted was for me to feed him and coo over him and fluff up his pillows like a good nurse. Plus, you can't ever really hate a sick person—it would be like hating a little kitten, the kind that stumbles around all blind, mewling for its mother.

Best of all, while he was sick, *everyone* came to visit him. Clara even moved into one of the guest rooms because she thought I needed the help. Everyone wanted to talk to me, to hear about how hard Benji's illness was on me and how worried I was about our future together. I cried when I mentioned that we'd only had one good year together.

Then, I let him get a bit better, spacing out his episodes to maybe one or two per month. Man, it was hard to do that! I got so bored in that big old house with just Benji for company, and sometimes it took all the willpower I had not to make him sick again, if only for a little break from the ordinary.

I did it, though. I restrained myself and, as soon

as I could, I got Benji to draw up an insurance policy for me. By that time, it wasn't too hard. I had put a little bit of a scare into him, health-wise, and I knew he wanted to make sure that I was looked after when he was gone.

Benji liked that about me, how I needed someone to provide for me.

"You're no working woman," he told me once, with a little chuckle in his voice. I knew he thought he was being really smart with that, like he was insulting me without letting me know that he was insulting me. But I *wasn't* a working woman or, if I was, my job was much more lucrative than some dumb nine-to-five.

The secret to my really good insurance contract, though, was allowing him to get almost back into fighting shape before we drew up the papers. In fact, the day before we went to see his lawyer, we'd hiked Laurel Canyon together. "Not so bad for an old fella," he'd said when we got to the top. He'd made me take eight different pictures of him up there, so I'd known he was pleased with himself.

A little bit of fear and a lot of confidence, that was the trick. He'd gone into the insurance meeting thinking that it was a necessary formality, not something that I would need for many, many years. It was a very favorable policy, and now—finally!—it was time to cash in.

I really hoped that everyone would appreciate all the work I did. This was my first real party for rich folks, and there were all these rules about how you should show off your money. If you showed it off in the wrong way, then that was bad and you exposed yourself as some kind of peasant. I'd gone to nine different bakeries before I found one that wasn't too "undiscovered" but also wasn't "over-exposed." Nine! I'd spent two days on the phone trying to get the right kind of string band!

And, while I was doing all of this, I'd had to keep an expert eye on Benji's crowshood dosage. I wanted him to feel just a little bit off, like something was coming up on the horizon, but not so sick that he was truly worried or—God forbid!—asked to cancel the party.

Now, though, his party was on Saturday and absolutely *everyone* was coming and all my hard work would be rewarded.

* * *

The cake—well, *cakes*—was a little ostentatious, Clara had to admit. But she never would have said anything like that to Julien. The poor little thing tried so hard! And "poor" was the operative word.

Benji never said much about where Julien had come from, and Clara had the impression that Julien herself hadn't exactly been forthcoming, but it was clear to anyone with eyes that she wasn't used to the kind of lifestyle that Benji and Clara had been raised in.

Still, she gave it everything she had, fluttering around to all of the guests to make sure that their glasses were full and everyone got a slice of that really quite hideous cake (she'd had someone do a rendering in icing of a photo of the two of them, and it made Benji look like some sort of aged goblin in the process of kidnapping a fairytale princess).

And Julien looked the part of the princess herself that night, in a dull pink dress with a heart cut over her chest. Her hair was in perfect loose coils, and she had a low-makeup look that Clara envied. Some girls just had all the blessings.

Benji, by contrast, was not looking so good. Clara had been so happy when he finally got married (even if they did do it on a wild spur, telling no one and having no celebration). She didn't like the thought of him sitting alone in that big house, becoming more and more the faded playboy with every passing year. Julien was good for him, an injection of life. And it wasn't too late, Clara thought, for the two of them to pop out a few kids. After all, Benji and Clara's father had been nearly sixty-four when Clara was born. The big house could use some little feet to make it noisy and busy again.

But it had been more than a year now and, instead of new life, it seemed that Benji had taken a hard turn for the worse. Sometimes Clara even wondered if it was the marriage that had accelerated his aging process. Perhaps the comfort and security of finding someone to love had made him give up on the diet and exercise regimen that he had sustained for so many years?

She didn't think Julien would allow that, though. Sweet though she was, Julien surely wanted the youthful, handsome older man she had married, not some frail husk.

In contrast to his wife, Benji barely moved during the party. In fact, he frequently seemed to forget that a party was going on, and he would start looking around him in bewilderment for a few moments before settling into a placid, unseeing expression.

Julien had set him up on the sofa and, periodically, she would flutter back over to him to adjust his blankets or bring him food (which he didn't touch) or just kiss his forehead fondly.

It was that sort of care that had brought Clara around on the matter of Julien. When Clara's brother first told her he had up and married a woman more than forty years younger than himself, she had been horrified. She knew it was unfair to stereotype but she couldn't help but be wary of this beautiful girl who clearly came from nothing and now wanted to marry into enormous wealth.

It helped when she found out that Julien had been married before (to a Wealth Consultant of all things) and presumably she had ample resources supplied by her now sadly deceased husband. But it was really the tenderness that Julien had toward Benji that convinced Clara her heart was in the right place. Where another woman might have run screaming, Julien seemed to thrive. No task was too embarrassing or disgusting for her to tackle and she did it all with a smile on her face.

Besides, Clara knew that her own brother was no

fool when it came to such things. In fact, Clara had thought for years that Benji had veered too far in the other direction. He'd dated many women, some of them quite seriously, but he seemed to have an almost pathological resistance to marriage.

Things changed, though, as one aged. You started to become less concerned about people depending on you, burdening you, and you began to worry more about depending on someone, about being taken care of. And Julien was a natural caregiver. Through all of Benji's illnesses she was utterly stalwart, never anything less than cheerful. After she had spent hours nursing him and looking after his every need, she would snuggle in next to him as though there were nowhere else in the world she would rather be. As incredible as it seemed, that little girl really, truly loved her husband.

"Can I sit with you?" Clara asked, taking up a seat on the sofa where Benji was stationed. He did not so much nod as just allow his chin to sink deeper into the blankets tucked around him, but Clara took that for an agreement.

"Sixty-eight," she said, reaching out to take his hand. It was cold and uncomfortably damp, like the hand of someone who had died in water. She squeezed his hand and he attempted to return the gesture but his grip was weak. "You've beaten mother, at least."

Benji made a laugh-like sound. Up close, Clara could see that someone (Julien, it had to have been Julien) had applied makeup to Benji's face with an expert hand. He was wearing a matte powder that gave his skin a warmer color than it would have had otherwise.

The laughing sound had turned, becoming rough and wheezy. "Benji, are you okay?" Clara peered down at his face, barely visible in the depths of his blanket. His eyes were huge and his pupils blown out like a coke fiend's.

Clara pulled the blankets away from his face,

revealing his tiny, sunken frame. Had he really lost that much weight since she had seen him last?

Benji grabbed her wrist with what must have been all his strength. He sucked useless air in through his mouth, lips tinged an uneasy purple, and something inside of him crinkled and rasped like discarded plastic. He was trying to say something to her but could not get the words out. His hand on her wrist felt like a chilly bracelet—loose and fragile.

Was this what dying looked like?

"Help!" Clara called out, loud enough to be heard over the band, who stopped playing in stages: first the violinist, then the vocalist, finally the woman with her enormous bass cello. "Benji's having an episode!" she called out and the room turned toward her, discomfort almost palpable.

The crowd rippled and Julien appeared, shooing people aside as she raced over to Benji. Julien barely spared Clara a glance, but there was a moment—a fraction of a moment, really—when Julien looked at her and Clara thought she saw something so cold and poisonous on the young woman's face. But then the moment passed. Julien flew into action, digging a cell phone out of her purse and calling 911.

It must have been a trick of the light, Clara told herself, or just a strange half-expression, because why would Julien have any cause to look at her like *that*? Like she had never hated anyone so much?

2

Hell's Bells

A foul-smelling herb also called Jimsonweed.
Produces delirium, overheating, and racing
heart.

The man in Room 307 was fine, though there
was no telling his bimbo wife that. God, what a
cliché this woman was. The frothy yellow hair, the
long, bare legs, what was probably a modest C-cup
lifted and contorted into DDs. And the clothes!
Everything designer, everything so obviously
expensive and so cheap at the same time. She had a
cut-out shaped like a heart over the epicenter of her
cleavage, for fuck's sake.

I was surprised when Sandy, the nurse who was
training me, seemed so taken by her. Trophy Wife

was the type of girl that women usually hated. The kind who "coincidentally" always had only male friends and was probably fucking her mom's boyfriend by tenth grade. Her husband was pushing seventy and while he didn't look bad for his age, he was still an old man. She said she was twenty-five but that smelled strongly of bullshit to me.

And there was Sandy, the sort of pert, chubby girl who had about three years left where she could reasonably be called cute before she got truly fat, taking both the Trophy Wife's hands in her own and giving them a comforting squeeze. "You're doing just fine," she said while the Trophy Wife managed to produce a few perfect tears.

Didn't she realize that Trophy Wife had nothing but sad contempt for her?

Anyway, the old dude—her husband—probably had a bad flu that had dehydrated him. It was rough, sure, but it was nothing that a couple of days in the hospital couldn't cure. To hear Trophy Wife talk, though, he was on his damn death bed.

The worst part was, she was riling up the whole room with her bullshit. He had come in with a whole wagon train of people dressed for a summer gala or whatever and there were about nine people packed into his room, all looking anxious and muttering to one another.

"Whatever he needs, I want it," the Trophy Wife said. "Even if you have to send him to a better hospital, whatever it takes."

What it would take was an IV drip and some time to heal away from his histrionic arm candy, but no one asked the trainee-nurse. I must have had some look on my face (probably a "this is a bunch of bullshit" look) because Trophy Wife noticed me, apparently for the first time.

"This isn't a teaching hospital, is it?" she asked, sizing me up. She'd probably made me for a sharp person, not another one of these stupid rubes who would flatter all her delusions. Now she'd do everything she could to get me out of the room so I wouldn't infect everyone else with my good sense.

"I'm employed here," I said. "I'm just shadowing Sandy for today and I'll go into standard rotation tomorrow."

She just nodded, still looking pissy. "I'm sorry, I know I'm probably over-reacting here but . . . after I lost Jakob . . . " Her eyes started to shimmer and a small woman with a silver cap of hair put an arm around her.

"We're all a little raw," the silver-haired woman said. "Benji is so special to us."

"Of course, of course," Sandy said and I wondered if maybe I hadn't gotten her wrong. Maybe she wasn't taken in by Trophy Wife's little show, maybe she was just really good at telling families what they wanted to hear. If so, maybe I would learn an actual skill during this instructional period.

"We're gonna do everything we can for Mr. Fraye. He's in safe hands here," Sandy assured her, pulling me out of the room with her. As soon as we got out into the hallway, her face changed, becoming that neutral mask of efficiency all the nurses wore.

"Okay, we're going to keep a close eye on this one. This is his third hospitalization this year and he's in a compromised state."

"Did all those people come every time?" I couldn't imagine an entire family dropping everything in their lives to sit at a sick old man's bedside every time he farted sideways.

Sandy nodded. "Benji Fraye is rich as Croesus. They're probably all trying to keep their place in the will."

And none, I imagined, more than Trophy Wife in there. This must be a bonanza for her. Hubby was chronically ill and she was still young enough to get out there and find another poor bastard to suck dry.

⁂

As far as emergency room positions go, St.

Eustachius was a pretty cush one. I wasn't going to be spending my time stopping up bullet holes for gangbangers or picking maggots out of some homeless guy's wounds. No, St. Eu was more of a "Help, my South American butt implants are infected!" kind of place and that suited me just fine.

I had been the top of my class in nursing school with sterling recommendations from nearly every professor I'd had. It was a little easier for me to stand out as one of just a handful of male nurses in the program, but I had certainly distinguished myself with my work as well. That was why I'd landed such a nice position and that was why, eventually, I was going to head up the nursing department there at St. Eu.

For now though, I was keeping quiet, watching and learning, not drawing too much attention to myself. I figured I would be a target there soon enough—a guy working in a female-dominated industry was always going to have to deal with backbiting drama and straight-up sabotage from his co-workers—but I wanted to push that off as far into the future as possible.

As soon as my break started, I got my cell phone and checked my e-mail. Sure enough, there was more endless blabber from Deborah about her fantasy lawyer who was going to sue me for something; who the hell knew what.

Deborah was constantly pulling the same shit, making vague threats about getting "the authorities" involved if I didn't cease all contact with her. But who was the one who returned my texts and my phone calls, even if only just to yell incoherently? The other night, I took the long way home and went by her apartment and there she was, sitting on her sofa in just a sports bra with the front curtains drawn aside so anyone could see inside. You can't tell me she didn't know exactly what she was doing. I bet she sat there like that every night this week just waiting for me to drive by.

Girls like Deborah were laughably easy to game. They might piss and moan about it but, deep down, they wanted drama and excitement. They wanted a man who would pursue them with everything he had. When she finishes acting out whatever little play she's scripted here and we get back together, I guarantee you, it will be the best sex we've ever had.

I started to draft a reply to her right there in hallway. I didn't see the need to go to the break room because I wasn't eating or anything, just checking my phone, so I was caught off guard when someone poked me hard in the chest.

I almost dropped my phone and looked up at my assailant only to find her, the Trophy Wife. "I pressed the buzzer," she snipped.

"And I'm on my break." I said it before I could really think about it, before I could remember that I was lying low and that probably included not mouthing off to the patients' families. All things considered, though, she was pretty lucky all she got was a snotty answer. If she tried that shit when I was on my own time, I would have laid her out on the fucking floor.

"He's taking too many breaths in a minute," she continued, like I hadn't said anything at all. Of course, for people like her, I might as well just have been silent and unthinking, like a piece of furniture. No, I was more like an elevator or something—just a *thing* that existed to service her needs and had no life of its own.

"You want me to go in there and make your husband breathe less?"

She narrowed her eyes at me. Up close, I could see she really was good looking in the face, not just mocked up with contouring makeup and all that shit like a lot of allegedly "beautiful" girls. She had good bones, big eyes, even teeth. She could have been a model. Hell, she probably *was* a model before she realized that the big money was in trying not to look repulsed while some elderly creep grunted and thrusted on top of her.

Her nose looked like it had been broken at some point in the past and had never quite healed correctly. I was a little surprised that someone like her wouldn't have had that fixed right up as soon as she had the dough but it was actually a good feature on her. It was arresting; it drew in the eye and forced you to contemplate her eyes—a color between blue and green—and the absolutely perfect shape of her mouth. Maybe that was exactly why she never got it fixed; maybe she was a little smarter than the average bimbo.

"I want you to go in there and give my husband proper medical treatment. Which, frankly, seems like the least you can do, seeing as his grandfather's endowment paid for half this fucking building." She started out her little speech all quiet and carefully enunciating but I heard something in the latter half, something rough-edged and ignorant. A bar-skank cadence, a little bit of a *Cops* drawl, maybe.

"Sure thing, ma'am," I said in the sunniest tone I could muster. She looked at me too long and I knew she was seeing the disdain in my eyes.

"What's your name?" she asked, which was just

one step removed from "Can I speak to your manager?" in supercilious-bitch language.

"Everett Priest." I gave her a big smile.

"Everett? Move your ass."

She turned on her heel and walked back toward the old man's hospital room, a motion that sent her own ass swaying ever so slightly. She was the kind of girl you loved to see both leave *and* walk away.

"Ma'am?" I called out and she stopped in the door of her husband's room. "What's *your* name?" Two could play at this tattletale bullshit.

"Julien Fraye. *Mrs.* Fraye," she added, like anyone could forget. The dude she happened to be married to was the only thing that mattered about her.

. . .

Julien stood in the corner, just waiting for me to fuck something up. How the hell would she even know if I fucked something up, though? Her medical expertise probably began and ended with knowing roughly how to stick on a Band-Aid. But there she was anyway, glowering with arms folded so her breasts were pushed up into the cutout on her chest. Yeah, real intimidating, like getting stared down by a RealDoll.

The patient's breathing was slightly rapid, but nothing to be too concerned about. I asked him if he needed anything adjusted and he waved me away impatiently. I was standing in front of the wall-mounted television and it looked like he wanted to watch a golf tournament. He hardly seemed like a man in the throes a medical emergency. It was the biggest fucking TV I'd ever seen in a hospital room. I guess it paid to be a rich son of a bitch, but that went without saying.

"He's fine," I said.

"You barely looked at him."

"His condition hasn't changed. He's on antivirals and we're giving him lots of fluids. He's improved a lot since he came in. You don't have to be worried." I tried to ape some of Sandy's reassuring cadence.

"Are you supposed to be doing this alone?" She crooked one eyebrow, so goddamned proud of herself, like she'd just delivered the most cutting retort.

Of course I couldn't say anything because she was technically right. I was supposed to alert Sandy to anything like this, but I knew that Mr. Fraye was fine and I wasn't gonna waste Sandy's time with this crap.

"I have to go," I said. My fifteen-minute break was up anyway. I would have to wait until my meal break now to reply to Deborah. "It's a busy hospital. I have a lot of other patients to see." No matter how much money her husband had, I certainly wasn't going to just lay down and let her walk all over me, pretending my time was worth so much less than hers.

She didn't say anything but I knew what was going on in her hamster-sized brain. Women like her have tissue-paper skin and my failing to treat her like a princess would feel just like me spitting in her face.

I could sense it, that unearned anger. It followed me out of the room like a smell.

•　•　•

The next hour and a half was all pretty normal first-day stuff. We saw the idiot son of a state senator who had hit himself in the thigh with a nail gun while tripping balls. Then there was the chick from that reality show about the art gallery or something who needed the gallon of vodka and bottle of pain-killers pumped out of her stomach. There were a few more normal people, too. A couple more flu cases, a car accident and, of course, a full complement of junkies trying to scam meds.

Then the beeper on Sandy's belt started sing-ing, summoning us to Benji Fraye's room again. It hadn't even been ninety minutes, but the man in the bed was transformed. His skin was an unnerv-ing green-gray and the front of his hospital gown was covered in fluffy white sputum. He was clearly struggling for breath, clawing at his throat with far more strength that I would have imagined the old bastard had in him.

A closer nurse already had the crash cart on hand and a doctor, a reedy dude not much older than me, was working on him. Mr. Fraye was gurgling and writhing and nothing the doctor was doing seemed to help. I could hardly see through the tangle of people, but it looked like they'd already intubated him, which meant it wasn't an airway problem. It looked like his respiratory system was just shutting down altogether.

Most of his entourage had cleared out now. Only Julien was left and I could imagine the fit she threw when they tried to get her to leave. She had her hands over her mouth, fingers trembling slightly, watching the action.

She must have sensed that someone was looking her way, because she turned and caught my eye and, I swear to God, she smiled at me.

She fucking *smiled* at me. Like she had proved something, like she had won something.

It was over so quickly I almost convinced myself that it hadn't happened at all. Then, I saw the doctor stiffen up and raise his hands away from Fraye's body. Anyone who'd spent any amount of time in a hospital knew what that meant and Julien Fraye apparently knew what it meant as well.

She started wailing as soon as the doctor turned to look at her and opened his mouth, but I had been watching; I had seen her in the few seconds when no one was watching the grieving widow. I had seen her glow for just a moment, like a lightbulb burning out. She was triumphant.

3

Devil's Bread

Commonly known as hemlock or poison hemlock. Paralyzes the respiratory system and causes death via oxygen deprivation to the brain.

That bitch stole my fucking moment.

It was all perfectly planned. I had just brought out the cake and I was having the chef light all of Benji's candles, then I was going to go over to help him to his feet. There, I would discover that he wasn't breathing and cry out for someone to call an ambulance. I even picked my dress out specifically so it would provide the highest contrast with the dove-gray sofa. No one would have been able to look away from me.

Instead, stupid fucking Clara started squawking at least five minutes too early and threw off the whole thing. Who cares about the *second* person to rush to someone's side? Suddenly, I was the one calling the ambulance and Clara was the one having hysterics. Someone even came up and wrapped a blanket around her. A blanket! Why the fuck should she be cold?

Things started to get back on track in the ambulance (only I was allowed inside; Clara and a few other family members had to take their own cars). The EMT was getting misty as I told him all about how we hadn't even been married a full two years yet and how much I needed my Benji.

Our doctor wasn't looking to solve any medical mysteries, which is exactly what I like in a doctor. The nurse was really nice; she held my hand and brought me hot cocoa from the vending machine. She was sort of a big-sister type and she told me what a good wife I was being and how lots of people came in there without anyone at all.

That was true. If I had never met Benji, he probably would have died alone at home in one of his fourteen empty rooms. It was a gift, really, what I was doing for him. He was surrounded by everyone who had ever loved him and they were all looking at him and talking to him and making sure he was comfortable all the time.

Unfortunately, the nurse had a real asshole hanging on her apron strings. Ugh. This fucker. He was definitely the kind of kid that tied firecrackers to more than a few cats' tails. And he hated me, I could see it in that little hint of a sneer he couldn't keep off his face.

I knew exactly what he saw when he looked at me: every girl who'd ever turned down his offer of a drink at a bar, every hot chick in high school who fucked athletes and ignored him, his mother, his sister, every girlfriend he'd had, every female boss he'd secretly hated. The fact that I existed in the world, just being alive and not fucking him, made him light up with rage like a pinball machine.

I could tell the other nurse didn't like him much either; I saw her grimace in frustration when he butted in with some useless opinion. "As a man over sixty-five, he's in a higher risk bracket when it comes to the flu," he said, like she didn't know how the fucking flu worked or how old her patient was.

Fortunately, I didn't plan to spend much time in this hospital at all.

.   .   .

After what happened with Jakob, I told myself that I was never going to dose someone out of emotion again. The only way to do it right—to do it well—was to have a plan and keep to it.

That's all fine. It's great to have rules and everything but it's a little bit harder to adhere to them when there's some prick looking at you like you're something he stepped in.

This asshole—this Everett Priest—who the fuck did he think he was, trying to pull some power-play shit on me? Benji was in a corner suite, three times the size of an ordinary hospital room. He had no roommate, a private bathroom with a therapeutic bath, and his meals were provided by a boutique catering company that had partnered with the hospital. That was the great benefit of money—no one got to tell you what to do, no one got to sneer at you and make you feel small.

I wasn't really throwing the plan away, though, giving Benji his last dose now instead of in a day or two. I was just sort of accelerating it a little. He had selected a kind of bread pudding dessert from that fancy menu, and sweet things were good for putting wild crowshood in. It could have a little bit of a flavor sometimes. If it was a big dose, it needed to hide inside something stronger.

Benji had barely said anything to me since we arrived at the hospital. As far as I knew the crowshood didn't have any brain-damaging properties, but I had been dosing him for a long time and I couldn't help but wonder if his mind had gone wandering. All he wanted to do was watch the stupid television and he barely looked at me.

They had offered me one of those fold-up cots to sleep on, but I was insisting upon sleeping on the little sofa thing they had over by the window. That was the better picture, all things considered—devoted wifey curled up in an uncomfortable spot, holding a vigil all through the night at her husband's side.

I was going to have pass that up, though, because Benji wasn't going to make it through the night.

I made up the powdered crowshood myself—I pride myself on it, in fact. I went out and found the plants growing wild and picked them with my own hands, I dried them in bundles hanging from the ceiling (funny but I never had to lie about those; Benji thought it was cute how domestic and old-timey I was, drying my herbs in the kitchen). I crushed them into a fine powder with the mortar and pestle Mommie gave me. She said it had belonged to the women in our family for hundreds of years, and all over the surface it was shadowed with stains from a hundred, a thousand, different projects and preparations.

I put the powder in a little packet—it looked kind of like a tea bag if you weren't looking too closely—and I carried it around with me everywhere. It was comforting, like a handgun but without all the paperwork.

I mixed up Benji's bread pudding for him, taking the packet from my purse and tearing off a corner. I sprinkled it on top of the dish like cinnamon or sugar and he didn't even glance over at me. I suppose that's one thing I miss about Benji—how completely he trusted me.

Weighed against everything I stood to gain when he died, though, I could live without it.

"Here," I told him, pushing the bowl into his hands, "you didn't touch your dessert."

He waved an impatient hand at me. He was improving rapidly with the hospital's intervention but his throat was still pretty raw from the coughing and the wheezing, so he preferred not to speak, which was fine by me.

"You like bread pudding," I said. It was probably true. "And you didn't get to have any of your cake."

"C'mon," I wheedled and that finally drew his attention, pulling his eyes away from the TV. I looked at the bread pudding meaningfully. "Let's celebrate for real now."

He gave me his indulgent look, like he was a doting dad who just couldn't help giving his princess every little thing she wanted.

He took the bowl from my hand and raised a big spoonful to his mouth. He smiled when he ate it. He must have tasted nothing but the sugars, the vanilla, the cream—all the sweet and smooth and best parts with none of the bitter. That was not too bad, I think, as far as dying goes. I can think of a lot worse ways. I've seen worse ways, in fact.

* · * ·

I erred on the side of caution, really loading up the pudding with crowshood because I didn't want to wait too long. I wanted to make sure Fuckface was still on shift when all of this went down.

My efforts were rewarded about forty-five minutes later, when Benji's lungs began to shut down. I guess they have a real name for it, the sound that he made: the death rattle. That's not just a thing people say in old-fashioned movies, it's a real, clinical phenomenon. It happens when a body can't deal with fluids—you know, spit and snot and all those horrible things our bodies make all the time—and just drowns in it all.

His chest was jumping up and down. When I was a little girl, I used to try to catch the field mice that would creep their way into the cabin in the winter. Sometimes, I got lucky and actually got one. When I held them in my hands, I was always amazed by how rapidly their little bodies moved, in and out and in and out, their little rib cages swelling and deflating. I realize now that they were probably scared (or whatever mice feel) and their bodies were vibrating with adrenaline.

Benji was moving like that.

He reached out for me, like Jakob had in the bathroom of the hotel where he died. I went over to his bedside and grasped his hand. I realized there were tears in my eyes and I hadn't even had to work at summoning them up.

When I touched his hand, though, he did a funny thing. He pushed me away—at least, as much as he could manage when his lungs were filling up with water. He batted at my hand, weak but full of intention. He furrowed his brow at me. He didn't want my hand, he didn't want my touch.

Sometimes, dying people move in strange ways. Your brain doesn't die all at once, it flickers and flares, like a little kid playing with a light switch. Wires get crossed, impulses happen, bodies start to move all uncontrolled. They flail at the people they want to bring close and lash out when all they really long for is comfort.

That was what I was thinking before the doctor came in and I watched as Benji reached for him, clutched at his wrist and the sleeve of his coat like a little kid trying to convince his daddy not to leave without him. So it *was* comforting he was after but not from me. I felt a little flare of anger, hot in my belly. Wasn't that a fine way to treat someone who had always stood by him and had always taken care of him?

I got a handle on myself, though, took a deep, centering breath and started screaming.

"Help him," I cried to the doctor, who ignored me completely. That was perfect—if he had looked at me, it would have meant that I was doing something noteworthy, something other than what every other worried spouse would do.

The room seemed to suddenly sprout people, like those fast-motion videos of a plant blooming. Nurses, technicians, other doctors, they crowded me into the furthest corner of the room. I was trying to squeeze my way back to the center when I saw him again, trailing behind the other nurse with that stupid look on his face.

You see? I thought. *I told you he was sick and look at him now you arrogant fuck.*

He wasn't paying attention to Benji, though, not after that first moment when he came in the room and figured out what he was looking at. Instead, he was watching me, shooting me that dark look, his mouth all crumpled and pursed like the leaves of a carnation flower. I had the weirdest urge to blow him a kiss.

I satisfied myself instead with a smile, just one and very quick. It was only for him and he saw it, sure enough.

I was so engrossed, in fact, in our little pantomime that I almost missed it, that last moment when Benji stopped fighting and slipped away. It is amazing how quickly someone can go from being a person to a dead thing. It starts the moment your brain dies, maybe before. In a few hours, your face starts to change. Your skin takes on a thick, yellowish look, like you're carved out of an old-fashioned candle. You start to sink, with nothing underneath you to move and animate your muscles. Death reveals all the soft places and the holes.

The doctor looked at me. I was crying already but I made a long, tortured wail. I heard Mommie make that sound when my father died and I knew even then as a little kid that it was the sound of loss. I taught myself how to reproduce it just for moments like these.

A nurse came over and put her arms around me. In the doorway, Clara had finally appeared. She was looking at the scene in the hospital room with utter bewilderment. There was no despair on her face, just confusion. When the doctor moved away from the bed and she caught a glimpse of Benji lying there, not moving, not breathing, she gave an awful involuntary laugh.

She stumbled over to the bed, touching Benji's legs underneath his hospital blanket, and then his face. I knew what she would be feeling, how it would be colder than a living person's but not yet as cold as the dead's.

Then I turned and buried my face in the nurse's shoulder. I could allow my face to relax a little bit in her scrubs where no one could see.

· · ·

Oh God, that poor dumb kid, Sandy thought, reaching up to mechanically pat the girl's back. It was achingly clear to anyone looking how much she had depended on the old man.

She *was* young, though, and there would be plenty of time for her to figure things out. She'd have no problem finding someone else. Looking like she did, she'd probably have a line around the block the moment she crooked her little finger.

"You're gonna be okay," Sandy murmured, because it was the truth. This was a hard time, sure, but she had a lot of living left to do.

Sandy told herself what she always told herself

when she lost someone: we did what we could for him. And truthfully, after a while, she got a little numbed to death. Especially a death like this: older fella who went out with more money than God and all his family around him.

None of that would comfort the girl in her arms, though. Sandy was glad that the other woman, the older woman who was some kind of relative to the dead man, was there. She could reach out, offer a little bit of guidance to a kid trying to figure out how to live in the world.

It would have actually been pretty nice if the older woman had stepped up now, in fact. Sandy didn't have anything against offering some comfort to the bereaved but an ER nurse couldn't really stand around dispensing hugs all day.

She tried to catch the older woman's eye over the girl's head but the old lady was glued to Fraye's bedside. She was touching his hands, inspecting them.

Sandy looked over her shoulder at her trainee. He had a weird, lost look on his face like he was daydreaming or something. She figured that if he'd gotten this far in his training, then this could not possibly the first time he'd seen someone go out. But that wasn't really how he looked, not upset exactly. More like he was trying to remember something important that he'd forgotten.

Maybe he was. Maybe he was trying to reconstruct a grocery list in his head. He had a coldness about him, the new kid. When he showed up today, Sandy'd had a bad feeling that he was one of *those* types. Men who overcompensated for going into a traditionally female occupation by being more macho than thou and dismissing (sometimes subtly, sometimes openly) the advice and opinions of their female colleagues. At the very least, he had failed to charm anyone so far. Nina on day duty said he had a "real panty-sniffing vibe" and Elise (who was hired on right before him) said it seemed like, at any moment, "he was going to start talking really intensely about his gym routine."

He seemed to have made a connection with the

older woman, though, because she was looking right at him now, the body of Benji Fraye lying still in between them. Something—something that Sandy could not identify—was passing between the two of them. Priest still had that strange searching look on his face and the older woman seemed like she might be sick. Maybe she had a touch of Mr. Fraye's flu?

4

Naked Lady

Similar in appearance to a crocus, similar in effect to arsenic.

She'd killed him.

I'm not sure how and I don't know exactly why (though I can make a pretty educated guess) but I knew as soon as I saw that awful, smug smile on her face, Julien Fraye had killed her husband. I bet she didn't feel a single thing when she did it either (except maybe a little bit of downstairs excitement; I'd read about people like that, who got off on murdering).

Looking around the room, I could see that I was pretty much alone in my assessment, except for the old woman. She was a dusty old-money type and she probably spent the most time fluttering around Fraye, next to Julien of course. She was looking at Julien now like something was slotting into place for her and she didn't look happy, not happy at all.

Sandy practically pushed me out of the room before I had a chance to . . . signal the older woman or something, get her alone and away from Julien.

Sandy was talking at me out in the hallway, but I only heard a word here or there. "Rotation," "linen," "cremation."

"Wait," I interrupted, "who's being cremated?"

"Benji Fraye, apparently," Sandy paused outside a door to check the chart.

"What, no autopsy or anything?"

She twisted her mouth at me like she was trying not to laugh. "He had the flu and he was an old guy. It's not a big mystery."

"But isn't it just standard?"

Sandy shrugged. "With rich people, nothing is standard. The wife made Mr. Fraye's wishes very clear."

I'm sure she did. "So we just . . . let that happen?"

"Uh . . . yeah, we pretty much do. Handling the bodies isn't really your job, you know. We have enough to do just dealing with the living folks." She was definitely laughing at me now, I could hear it in her voice.

"Sure, makes sense." I nodded vigorously and generally tried to look like the kind of obedient flunky who would consider the matter completely closed now that Sandy had deigned to pass her judgement.

"Since you're so connected to this patient, why don't you do the laying out? I'll show you where the supplies are," Sandy said. I couldn't tell from the tone of her voice whether this was supposed to be a punishment or a genuine olive branch. Either way, I wasn't in a position to turn her down.

•   •   •

Ideally, we were supposed to lay out the body before the family saw it. Dying was hard on a body. This was supposed to make it easier, brushing the dead person's hair, putting them in fresh clothes. I don't know about that and, in this case, it seemed extra pointless since the widow and the sister were right there for the final moments.

Someone had ushered them out by the time Sandy and I came back with the supplies (a safety razor, a comb, a clean hospital gown, a plastic water basin, toothbrush and toothpaste). Benji Fraye was just as the doctors had left him—his chest damp with fluids, the sheets a tangle around him.

"Have at it," Sandy said. "I gotta get back out on the floor."

If this was her attempt at putting me in my place, she was shit outta luck because I have never had a problem with dead people. They've certainly caused me a lot less trouble than live ones.

I pulled the sheets and blankets off the bed, setting them aside for the laundry, and wrestled

Benji's gown off him. I don't know if it was the being naked or the being dead, but he looked much smaller lying there on the stripped mattress. His chest had the sort of withered look of someone who had been in shape for many years but couldn't halt the aging process. His skin was thin and violent-looking; bruises trailed up and down his arms from the IVs.

I wonder who did this for my dad. He died in the hospital, so someone must have done it. Someone like me.

I wiped Fraye's body down and taped new dressings over all his IV puncture marks. You're supposed to do that so the family can pretend that their loved one suffered no injuries as they passed. I wondered what Julien would think about that. Maybe she would prefer to see the blood and bruises?

I was brushing his hair when I heard someone in the doorway behind me. "Sorry, I'm not quite done yet," I said, before turning around to see the old woman standing there looking like she'd wandered into the wrong room.

She didn't acknowledge me as she approached Benji, her forehead wrinkling up like she was trying to solve a math problem in her head. "It doesn't seem real," she said, not necessarily to me. "That he's dead. He was just alive. Just a couple of hours ago."

I wasn't sure what she wanted me to do (if anything). I couldn't finish my work either because she was in my way. And what was I supposed to do, muscle a grieving woman aside so I could make sure her dead brother's mustache was neatly combed? So I just stood there, being dumb.

"I wonder about . . . if we'd done something differently. If I could go back, not even very far . . . maybe I could have . . . " She kept trailing off into silence, staring down at her brother.

"It was the flu," I offered. "There wasn't anything anyone can do . . . right?"

I gave her a little sidelong glance, trying to gauge

whether she had gotten my insinuation and whether she was offended by it. For the first time, her eyes seemed to focus and she looked at me like she was really seeing me.

"My dad passed away from something similar," I said, choosing every word carefully. "Of course, for us it was a little different. We weren't sure exactly what happened. My stepmother was . . . a pretty erratic person."

"That must have been very hard," the woman said. Her voice was so measured that there was no way of knowing whether she was just making polite conversation or trying to say something more meaningful. "When did you begin to suspect that something . . . irregular had happened?"

There it was. I knew it, I knew she felt the very same things I'd felt when I looked at Julien Fraye. "For me, it was just my stepmother's behavior and her character. I knew she wanted more from my dad than just companionship."

The woman made a "hrm" sort of noise.

"Sometimes we trust people before we really even get to know them. Sometimes we trust people because someone we love trusts them."

The woman was still silent. I started to worry that I had maybe misread her somehow.

"Julien isn't a selfish person," she said finally, softly. "She's a self*less* person. She took such good care of him. That's what everyone always said about the two of them. That she took such good care of him."

"Sure . . ."

"Did you ever find out exactly what happened to your dad?"

"Not for certain. I wasn't . . . around when he died. I couldn't get things checked out."

She reached down and touched her brother's hand the way she had just after he died. "It's hard," she said, "not knowing." Her voice was getting thick and I could see the skin around her eyes turning pink. "He's cold now."

I put my hand on her shoulder. She didn't flinch

away, so I figured she found it comforting. "I'll take care of him," I said. "That's my job."

• • •

"What? No." The head nurse, Mariah was a pencil-thin Mexican woman in her forties. She looked like the sort of person who put a lot of energy into looking busy all the time. True to form, she made me follow her around while I tried to address my concerns about Benji Fraye. "That's not your job, why are you getting involved?"

"I just want to make sure that no mistakes are made."

She rounded on me, narrowing her eyes. "Are you saying we made a mistake?"

"No. Not *us*. Just—I mean—I'm just trying to be thorough."

"Because Mr. Fraye was a very big-deal patient. If there were *any* suggestion of negligence involving him, that would also be a big deal. The kind of deal that gets people fired. Or sued."

Jesus, did this woman have any middle gears?

"So," she continued, not even pausing to let me answer, "before you start stirring the shit, I would just like you make sure that you have really, *really* good reason to get involved in this."

"I . . . just think that there might be something else going on."

"You *think*." Her voice was full of contempt. "And what makes you think that?"

"The behavior of the wife, some of the things she's said . . . " I trailed off, not wanting to admit that, more than anything else, I had just seen something in Julien. A cold viciousness beyond the typical gold-digging.

"So, because you don't like a woman, because you don't think she acts right, we should supersede the family's wishes and withhold a man's body, which I'm sure they wouldn't protest at all? And the media definitely wouldn't get involved with something like that. But, I mean, you've got a bad feeling and you've been here almost a whole day now, so we gotta honor that."

If she were a man, I would have hit her and no one could have blamed me for it. She wouldn't be expecting it either—women always thought they had a free pass to mouth off to their heart's content and no man would dare respond. I'd break her teeth on my knuckles, I'd put her down like a dog.

"Are we done?" she demanded

"Yup!" I said, smiling so hard it hurt.

• • •

Mariah must have told Sandy (and the whole rest of the gaggle) about me trying to leapfrog her because they were all giving me hateful looks. I could have pushed it even harder, tried the next level of authority up, but I didn't think it would do any good. Doctors didn't give a shit about what nurses thought most of the time and they gave even less of a shit what a new nurse thought. I had no way to access any board members or people with real power. But that didn't mean I was entirely out of options. Sometimes, if you can't go up, you gotta go sideways.

Lucy, the morgue attendant, had an unfortunate collection of features: a very long, very thin neck, a prominent, beaky nose, and huge round eyes. Any one of those in isolation would be inoffensive, even attractive, maybe, but altogether they gave her the unsettling look of a humanoid Big Bird. I knew she liked me, though. She did that thing women do when they sort of tighten themselves up and try to be as small as they can, like they're pretending to be some cute little animal.

I took it for granted that I could nail her; the real test would be getting a non-sexual favor out of her. Especially one that could jeopardize her career. She jumped when I knocked on the door, which I thought was a little fragile for someone who spent all day with dead bodies.

"Oh," she said when she saw and her face went stoplight red. I like it when girls have a strong blush response—makes it a lot easier to see how I'm doing.

"Hey Lucy," I said. She would like that I remembered her name; I bet lots of people didn't. "How are you?"

"I'm good," she said slowly, a little skeptically. Doctors and nurses probably never went down there unless they had to and I was guessing she didn't have a bunch of dudes following her around, hounding her for dates either. "What's up?"

I shrugged. "I lost my first patient today." I tried to look a little haunted (but not too broken up, no one likes an overly sensitive guy). "Mr. Fraye?"

Her eyes softened like taffy in the summer sun. "I'm sorry, that's really hard."

I pulled my lips into my mouth like I was having a problem keeping it together. "I guess I just feel like . . . I might have done something, you know? Done something different?" I thought back on the sister's words, how she wanted to go back and change things.

Somehow, Lucy softened even more. "That's really common," she said. "Especially for your first time."

I went over to where she was wiping down a long metal table and allowed her to put a comforting hand on my forearm. "But I'm sure you did everything right."

"He's down here now, huh?"

She nodded. "We're just waiting on the guy from the funeral home to pick him up."

I glanced behind me at the wall of refrigerated drawers where the dead were held in a brief limbo before the family decided what was going to be done with them. "I just . . . I wish I knew more. Had that little bit of closure."

Lucy nodded again but she was a little hesitant now, like she was trying to figure out exactly where I was going with all of this. "So, he isn't going to the coroner then?" I asked.

"Um . . . no? Not that I heard."

I tried to sound as casual as possible. "I just thought there were some questions. I wasn't sure." Lucy was a good three inches shorter than me. I looked down in the general direction of her tits until her throat started getting all pink again. "That's a nice necklace," I said, reaching out to touch the small silver ankh she had on a leather loop around her neck. Lucy never grew out of her teenage goth phase.

She laughed too hard and it had a jittery edge to it, like it was going to get away from her at any moment and turn into one of those crazy witch cackles. I realized that, by paying even this scanty amount of attention to her, I was risking a barrage of thirsty Facebook chats and increasingly dire text messages. "Thank you," she said, leaning slightly into my hand.

"I kinda wish he was going to the coroner," I said and Lucy's eyes were big and dumb. She wasn't hearing a word I was saying, probably decorating our future house and naming our non-existent kids in her head. "Just so I could be sure. You know. That I didn't screw something up."

I smiled at her. I have been told that my smile is my best feature, or one of them at least.

"Um," she began uncomfortably, "well . . . there are some things that we can do here in the morgue. Not like a full autopsy," she added quickly.

"Oh, of course not!"

"Just, like, some tests."

"Like blood and tissue tests," I provided.

"Yeah . . . " her voice was slow and doubtful. I reached out and put a warm hand around her arm. She was shivering, though it was actually pretty temperate for a morgue. "I, I can do that for you." She turned her shining face toward me and smiled a smile that had far too much gum to it.

"You're a doll, Lucy," I said, dipping my head to kiss her cheek.

5

Bloodroot

Sanguinaria canadensis, so named for the thick, red juice is produces. Kills animal and human cells on contact.

The funeral was critical for me. It was my debut as a widow and an opportunity to cement myself in the minds of the city's rich and important. It wasn't easy, though, with Clara nosing her way in and questioning every damn thing I did. First the urn was too big (of course it was big! People were going to look at that and know someone who mattered was inside), then she didn't want to have a reception at all. I pointed out how weird that would look but she was barely listening to me.

Then she started fighting me on the cremation.

I told her that she was too late, which was sort of a half-truth. I did get Benji out of the hospital fast—four hours after he died, he was safe in the mortuary's hands—but I probably could have halted the cremation if I'd really wanted to, which I did not.

People get so irrational around death. They forget how to act in their best interests and start clinging to all this dumb stuff that doesn't matter at all. Like, Clara was trying to tell me that we shouldn't try to sell the summer house on Westfall Island in North Carolina when this was the best buyer's market in a decade.

She was lucky she had me around. I was the one who did an inventory of all of Benji's accounts; I was the one who had bothered to get power of attorney six months ago when he had a really bad spell; I was the one who was contacting real estate agents, money managers, life insurance companies, and did I get so much as a single fucking "thank you"? Of course not. I just got more whining.

"Julien?" she said my name on the phone like it might have been someone else. I'd moved into the Four Seasons after Benji died, which I said was because I couldn't bear to be in the house alone. It was mostly true; I'd always been a little lonely and a little restless in the mansion. In the hotel, I could always head down to the bar when I needed to see a friendly face. All faces were friendly when I walked into a room. At first.

More importantly, getting out of Benji's house was the first step in getting out of town. Did you ever see that old game show where they let folks— curly haired, pudgy housewife-types—go running like crazy through a supermarket just pulling shit off the shelves, trying to fill up a cart before the buzzer went off? That was how I planned to deal with Benji's money.

"Hi, Clara." I tried to match her slow, subdued tone when I talked to her. I could tell, sometimes, from the way that people looked at me when I talked about Benji dying that I wasn't sounding exactly right.

"Did you file a claim on Benji's life insurance?"

Here we go, this fucking Chinese finger trap of a question. People always act like collecting on an insurance policy is the worst, most heartless thing a person can do when their husband dies, but that's exactly what an insurance policy is for. Right then, I needed to *ensure* that I got my money before some overzealous financial advisor swept in to lock all of Benji's assets up in the legal equivalent of Fort Knox.

"I did," I said. "Our lawyer said I should."

"But we don't even know how Benji died yet."

"Yes we do," I said immediately. "He died from the flu. From complications of the flu." I tried to sound relaxed and natural, but I could feel my heart speeding up, vibrating painfully under my ribs.

"Yes," Clara said, but she said it too slow and she waited too long. "I just think maybe we should . . . wait until things are clearer."

I wanted to scream at her that it was clear, it was Waterford-fucking-crystal clear. Benji was dead; he didn't need the money and I was alive and I needed it badly. What was there to wait on?

Instead, I made my voice as casual as I could manage. "Okay. I'll tell Franklin to put a hold on things." Benji's lawyer wasn't named Franklin and I didn't have a lawyer so, I suppose in the grand scheme of things, this wasn't really a lie.

"Thank you, Julien," Clara said, and there was that warmth in her voice again but I couldn't completely trust that now. I couldn't completely trust *her*.

"I'm so glad you're here, Clara," I told her. "I don't know if I could make it without you."

. . .

"What samples?" I asked and the idiot on the phone gave me a long wordless stutter. "My husband was cremated, there weren't any samples."

"I just . . . uh . . . I just have this list. My boss told me to call. Because the samples on this list are going to take longer and . . . I mean, this isn't really my thing. I don't test them or anything. I just call the people on the list because—"

"Because the samples are going to take longer," I snapped. "Yeah, got the gist. What are you testing these samples for?"

"Um . . . " he said again and I heard the sound of keys being tapped. "It looks like just for, like, irregularities and stuff."

"What are *irregularities and stuff?*"

"You know, like, elevated levels of chemicals that could indicate a medical problem. Toxins, that sort of thing."

Toxins.

Mommie was smart in so many ways, even though she only had what people would call a grade school education. I don't think she was smart enough, though, to know all about how medical labs tested for poisons and to find one that didn't show up. Even if I somehow got lucky, though, I couldn't afford to wait here, all exposed, while they finished testing.

"If I can ask, who ordered these tests?" It had to have been Clara. She'd gone behind my back, pretending to be all kind and sisterly when, really, she was just waiting to undermine me. Lying, two-faced bitch. She probably never liked me at all, some slutty peasant marrying into her illustrious family.

"Uh . . . " the voice on the phone said again. Who was this idiot, someone's stupid grandson who needed an after-school job? "I can't really tell. It looks like . . . the hospital sent it in, I guess?"

Clara had probably covered her tracks, made it look like standard procedure. "Okay," I said, "thank you for letting me know!"

As soon as I hung up the call, I started packing.

•　•　•

The apartment complex was the same as I

remembered, except they had finally closed the big, outdoor pool in the center. It was empty now and scattered with garbage, including what looked like a broken grocery cart.

Joanie still lived in the same unit, B17, and she still had the same welcome mat out in front of the door. It had a dense floral design and the word WELCOME was printed in dark red letters.

Joanie didn't open the door all the way when I knocked, she just cracked it and looked out at me, not surprised, and said, "No."

But she didn't close the door the rest of the way.

"I'm in trouble, Joanie," I said.

"You *are* trouble."

"Please," I said. I summoned some tears, just enough to make my eyes glassy. "Please, I really messed up this time."

She made me wait for a long moment, her face cloudy with disapproval before she finally stepped back, opening the door and rolling her eyes as she did it. "I swear, Ju—wait, what are you calling yourself these days?"

"Julien," I told her. "But I think I'm gonna have to change it pretty soon."

She sighed. "I can't keep up with you, girl."

I gave her a big ol' bear hug because I knew that was what she wanted from me, and she held herself stiff in my arms and tried to pretend she didn't like it. "Alright, alright," she said, breaking away from me. "You can crash here but just for the night. My girls are coming back from their dad's tomorrow and I don't want you here when they are."

That was crap. I was there when she had her first daughter, I was the *only one* there. I changed that kid's diapers and now she was gonna try to tell me that I was some bad influence? True, I hadn't known about the second one (I moved around a lot, Joan probably didn't have my new contact information) but if I had known, I would have come out to see her.

There'd be time later to soften her up, though. Joanie always softened up.

Joan's apartment was somehow even smaller than I remembered. It was an efficiency, which meant that it was basically just one big room, a tiny kitchen that spread seamlessly into a sort of living room, which Joan had divvyed up with a bunch of sheets hung up like curtains.

It was government housing, earmarked for kids coming out of foster care. It was supposed to help people transition into their adult lives but Joan'd had the place for a few years now and it didn't look like she planned on moving any time soon. There were coloring books open on the tiny kitchen table, brightly colored sponges in the bathtub, and a pink plastic tricycle packed into the corner.

"You can sleep in my bed," she said, "I'll get out a sleeping bag. You hungry?" she asked.

The sleeping bag she eventually produced was familiar, a scratchy green sealskin exterior and flannel insides. I'd had one just like it once but, unlike

Joan, I had left it behind when I left my foster home. She tossed it onto the living room floor next to a small pyramid of the knock-off Barbies you could buy at the dollar store.

Joanie wasn't that much older than me—three years—and we looked a lot alike. She had never been as pretty as I was and she had a little bit of sag from the pregnancies but she still looked okay. A hell of a lot better than some of the busted-looked hags I'd seen on rich mens' arms. I don't know if those women hooked 'em when they were younger or what but, if they could make it happen, Joanie could clean up.

She'd never do it though. In her mind, it was somehow nobler to work at the Taco Bell thirty hours a week and still need food stamps than to marry rich.

"I'm a little hungry," I said. "What you got?"

She raised her eyebrows at me. "What do *I* got?" she gestured at me in my Louboutins with the ring I'd gotten from Benji and its ruby the size of a kid's gum ball. "Your ass is buying dinner tonight, Princess."

I smiled. She was softening already.

* * *

Not shockingly, Joanie's ex had flaked on her, dumping the girls at her door a night early.

The big one's name was Albertine, I remembered that now. The little one was Miranda. Joan always liked those weird old fashioned names. I think she believed that it would give her girls some little boost up out of the crappy situation they'd been born into. Names weren't worth much, though. I knew that from experience.

"How come you are my aunt?" Albertine asked, twining a string of pizza cheese around her index finger.

"'Cause your mommy and I are sisters, just like you and Miranda are sisters," I said. Albertine looked sideways at Miranda, who was stuffed uncomfortably into a high chair that was just a little too small for her.

"Where's your mommy?" Albertine's eyes narrowed suspiciously. I almost laughed, she reminded me so much of myself when I was little.

Joan didn't let me answer her, though. "Gramma is gone, honey. She passed away before you were born."

Albertine nodded deeply. "How come I don't see you?"

"She means why hasn't she met you before," Joanie informed me, spooning a little bit of ooze from a plastic container into Miranda's mouth. Her pizza was sitting on a plate at her elbow, untouched.

"I don't live here," I told her. "I live far away. In a big city."

"Where is your baby?" Albertine continued, the tiniest interrogator. She had lost all interest in her pizza by this point and I wondered why I even bothered buying dinner for this family of ingrates.

"Huh?"

Joanie sighed, wiping a smear of food from Miranda's mouth with the side of her hand. Gross. "She wants to know where your children are. She thinks every woman over thirteen is a mommy."

I bit back a mean remark about how, considering Joanie's tender age when Albertine was born, that maybe that wasn't such a crazy assumption for the kid to make. But even I knew not to test my sister's hospitality that far.

"No babies for me," I said. Albertine seemed to find that an unsatisfactory answer, but she didn't say anything. Instead, she started pulling the crust off her pizza and tearing it into smaller and smaller chunks.

"If you're gonna eat, eat, don't play with it," Joanna snapped and I jolted a little bit in my seat. She sounded so much like Mommie (and how many times had I heard the very same thing at the dinner table?). Joanie gave me a look across the table and I wondered if she was thinking the very same thing I was.

I had forgotten how nice it felt to be with people who knew your way of thinking and who understood you. It was like Daddy always used to tell us, family is the only thing in the world that you can really trust.

· · ·

Albertine wondered if New Aunt knew Barbie for real. They looked the same, maybe they went to the same places.

She wasn't completely sure that the woman was her real Aunt. Sometimes, when she went to Daddy's house, there were ladies there who Daddy said were aunts to her but, most of the time, she never saw them again. Maybe New Aunt was like that.

Albertine didn't think New Aunt could really be Mama's sister because Mama didn't seem to like her all that much. Albertine didn't always like Miranda (she wanted a brother to play with not a baby sister) but she did most of the time (at least when Miri wasn't crying). But Mama was always looking at New Aunt, always watching her, and not like how she watched Albertine at the park, where she was just making sure that nobody bad came along and hurt them. Mama watched New Aunt like she *was* someone bad.

New Aunt took Mama's bed and Mama had to sleep on the floor. She told Albertine to come over and snuggle up with her and then she zipped the sleeping bag up around the both of them. She smelled like her hand lotion and the shampoo that Albertine liked to squeeze into her bath, even though Mama said that was wasting it.

Albertine scooched down in the sleeping bag until only her nose and eyes were peeking out. She rolled on her side, facing the bed where New Aunt was already sleeping. It was dark now but Mama had left on the nightlight and it lit up New Aunt, the edge of her nose and her long, yellow hair.

Albertine decided that she would watch her while

Mama slept. She would make sure that New Aunt didn't do anything bad. Albertine meant to watch all night but, before she knew it, her eyes were drooping and she was so warm in the sleeping bag with Mama's arm around her that she couldn't help it, drifting off into sleep.

6

Doll's Eyes

Flowering plant common in eastern North America. Produces unique white, round berries that give the plant its name. The berries are sweet and, if ingested, can paralyze the heart muscle in minutes.

Julien Fraye's social security number brought up a plethora of medical records. Most recently for Julien Hammersmith, who had come in with a broken nose and lacerations on her hands, before that for Julien Jones, who had gotten breast implants (shocker). Finally, and most interestingly, there was a record of young Emily Cherie Freeport being treated for "penetrating trauma by unknown item" in Indiana a few years ago.

I wasn't surprised that Julien had changed her name. It was exactly the kind of shady thing I would have imagined she'd done at least once. But it was important information all the same. Emily might have a paper trail where Julien, with the exception of the last three years, had nothing.

I made copies of all of this information to take back to my apartment and examine more closely later. I had to be careful because, technically, I wasn't supposed to have access to any of this.

Lucy had been on staff for eight years and had much more clearance than I did. She gave me her login information when I told her that I was worried about a patient (a seven-year-old girl who I made up entirely) and wanted to check her records for any other red flags.

Lucy trusted me and all it really took was a couple of coffee dates and one deeply unsatisfying sexual encounter. More than anything I did, though, Lucy *wanted* to trust me. She wanted to believe that a guy like me wanted a girl like her. I didn't even really feel like I was fooling her so much as I was just standing back and allowing her to fool herself.

When Benji Fraye's samples came back from the laboratory she'd sent them off to, I'd start the process of fading from her life. She would get the hint eventually and, even if she didn't, what could she do? That's why you can never give up all the power to someone else in a relationship—any relationship—because how are you going to yank them back when they decide to leave?

• • •

Emily Freeport had a rough life, even described in the dry, bureaucratic language of medical and psych reports, that much was clear. Her mom and dad ran a down-home meth lab out of their shitty trailer and her mom went to prison when Emily was in diapers. Her dad was about as good a parent as a raging meth-head could be—he trended toward neglect rather than all-out abuse—but she finally got taken out of his home after a police raid where cops found her smeared in her own filth, unfed, and unwashed amongst the open cans of paint thinner.

For a while she lived with a great-aunt, but then the old lady died and there was nowhere else to put her but into a group home. The group home environment didn't suit Emily, apparently, because she got bounced around a lot after a series of ominous-sounding "incidents" with the other kids. The last group home she lived in was more like a kiddie correctional facility than an orphanage. At some point, someone had seen fit to attach her entire DCS file to her medical records, probably in an attempt to get her on some anti-psychotics after she burned another girl with a pot of boiling spaghetti water.

The most interesting thing about Emily, though, was that I was pretty sure she died a decade ago.

It took some searching (and some pretty aggressive use of Lucy's log-in information) but I managed to find a death certificate signed by an Indiana coroner in Stanhoe County, a good six years before "Emily" showed up in an emergency room in Bloomington with what looked suspiciously like a gunshot wound.

So if Julien wasn't Julien and she wasn't Emily either, then who the hell was she?

•   •   •

Monday was my day off. I slept in late and woke up to thirty-eight texts from Lucy. She'd also called me more than a dozen times and emailed me as well. At first, I figured her crazy had just kicked in and I would have to ride it out for the next few days. I ignored the calls, deleted the texts and trashed the e-mails. She got me, though, by borrowing Sandy's phone. I didn't dare ignore a call from my boss (even just a temporary boss).

Before I even got the phone all the way to my ear, though, I could hear Lucy yelling. "What the fuck did you do? What did you do?" she kept demanding, not giving me any space to answer.

"Calm down—" I started.

"FUCK YOU, EVERETT! I'm gonna lose my job!" she shrieked into the phone.

Oh.

"Lucy—" She was sobbing. Crying was the last weapon in a woman's arsenal and every fight with a girl led inevitably to tears, just usually not this quickly.

"Look, I can't help you if you can't talk to me." Talking to women sometimes felt like trying to disentangle a dog from its own leash. *Just stop choking yourself, idiot.*

"What did you do with my log in?" she wailed. "They made me talk to a cop! They said the state health regulators might have to come in and do an investigation!"

"I didn't do anything," I told her. Technically, that was true. Someone using Lucy's name and login had accessed the medical files associated with Benji

Fraye and his wife Julien. It would only make sense to presume that person was Lucy herself. "Don't worry," I said, "this is probably some weird glitch in the system."

"It's just . . . everyone's talking about all this scary shit. Felonies and stuff. Lawsuits. Everyone's freaking out." She sounded slightly more subdued. As soon as I threw out an innocent explanation, no matter how flimsy, she had latched on to it hungrily.

"I really want to see you," she whined.

"I really do too," I said, opening up my laptop. I still had a number of documents related to Emily Freeport up and I paged through them idly while I half-listened to Lucy.

"Can I . . . come over to your place?"

"Sure," I said. "I'll text you the address." As if I'd ever tell that crazy bitch where I lived.

* * *

All of the addresses on file for Emily Freeport were

pretty normal. Group home to group home across Indiana, until the gunshot wound. For that procedure, she had given a P.O. Box in the tiny town of Deepwell, Indiana.

There was nothing in Deepwell, Indiana. I marshaled the entire power of the internet and all I could find was a two-and-a-half star Dairy Queen and some sort of summer corn festival. It wasn't until I searched Stanhoe County Group Home (the last place Emily was definitely alive) and Deepwell, Indiana that I hit upon it. It was one of those small-town puff pieces about patently uninteresting people who happen to live in the town, about this elderly couple who had been fostering kids on their farm for twenty years. There was a picture of them alongside the profile, with their then-recent crop of foster kids: a toddler of indeterminate sex, a little girl about six or seven, and a young teenager in a dumpy jean skirt. Her hair was pulled back in a ponytail and her chest was flatter than a sheet of paper, but I recognized Julien all the same. She was listed in the caption as *Allison Hunt, age thirteen.*

For one thing, it meant I was right about Julien pretending to be older. If this article was accurate, she was barely twenty. For another thing, this was pretty solid proof that she was up to something shady. If I showed this to Fraye's sister, she would have to admit that, at the very least, Julien had been lying since the moment she met them.

*   *   *

I knew as soon as I got to the central desk that something was wrong. Everyone was carrying themselves all stiff and weird, looking and me and trying to pretend like they weren't looking at me.

One of the other nurses I didn't know yet picked up the phone and muttered something quickly when I reached the desk. Like a really crappy magic trick, Mariah appeared along with a beefy dude I recognized as part of the hospital's security staff.

"Everett?" she said, and it seemed that everything about her voice and demeanor had changed. She was moving slowly and deliberately and talking like a kindergarten teacher. At any moment, she would ask me to put down the safety scissors.

I smiled. "Am I late?"

"Will you come with me?"

What else was I going to do? Go crashing through the front doors and steal a car from the parking lot?

Mariah took us to one of the bereavement rooms, a little enclosed space where doctors would take the families and friends when they had bad news to deliver. Inside the room, waiting for us, I guess, there was another guy. He was wearing jeans and a polo but I got a strong feeling of "cop" from him. He asked me to sit down on the little sofa there and pulled up a folding chair across from me. Mariah and the security guy hovered by the door like they weren't really sure if they were supposed to stay.

"Mr. Priest, what do you know about the recent

issues at the hospital with improperly accessed medical records?"

"Uh . . . I just got back. Yesterday was my day off," I said honestly. "I'm a little at sea with all this. What's going on?" The cop kept his face blank. I bet they have a class about how to do that at the police academy.

"So you know nothing about the medical records of Julien Fraye being hacked."

"Mr. Fraye's wife? No."

"But you remember Mrs. Fraye?"

"Sure. Mr. Fraye just died last week, it was my first day. Kinda memorable, you know?"

"And after that happened, did you talk to anyone about irregularities in Mr. Fraye's case?"

Fucking Lucy. She must have brought my name into this and then of course Mariah and Sandy would leap at the chance to make me look like a weirdo. "Irregularities?" I asked, pretending I couldn't possibly understand what he was talking about.

"Did you suggest to anyone that Mr. Fraye might not have died of natural causes?"

This could go two ways: I could completely deny everything and pretend that I had no suspicions about Julien. I would probably get fired (I had a feeling I was gonna wind up fired no matter what I did here) but they had no real proof that I'd looked at the medical records and it would just be the nurses' word against mine.

Or, I could tell the cop a strategically edited version of the truth and raise some of my issues with Julien and hope that he would see what I saw. I tried to size him up; he was forties-ish, military buzz, getting a little jowly—I bet he'd seen a lot of women like Julien in his lifetime. Vapid gold-diggers and slutty schemers were thick on the ground, especially in this town.

"I . . . did say something to that effect," I told him finally. "That I had concerns, I mean."

"About Mrs. Fraye?"

"About the whole situation," I corrected. "I just

thought with the very quick cremation schedule and Mr. Fraye's rapid downturn . . . well, it raised some red flags for me."

"But not for your supervisor?" The cop looked briefly over his shoulder at Mariah. It might have been my imagination, but it seemed to me that there was a little bit of judgement in that look, like maybe Officer Friendly here was thinking that I had some good instincts and was dismissed a little unfairly.

"No and so that's where I ended it. I know when I'm beat," I said, smiling at him. He did not smile back.

"So you didn't use Lucy Trembley's log in credentials to search the medical records database?"

I shook my head, baffled. "No, I mean, I may have talked about this to Lucy. Blowing off some steam, you know, but I never thought she'd do anything about it."

The cop raised his eyebrows, the first sign that any part of his face was actually mobile. "So Lucy Trembley did this without your knowledge?"

"I certainly didn't know anything about it."

"And Lucy decided to take samples from the body all on her own too, I bet?" Mariah interjected. The cop gave her a foul look and she clammed right the fuck up.

"I don't know anything about samples. I thought they didn't do an autopsy?"

The cop didn't say anything, probably didn't want to let on too much about the case. But if they knew about the samples, maybe they'd look seriously at the results.

"And what about Deborah Martinez?"

I felt a tingle of discomfort in my throat. Deborah didn't have anything to do with this. At least, she shouldn't. "Deborah is my girlfriend," I said. "I don't think she's very relevant to this."

"Your *current* girlfriend?"

"Yeah. We've been together eight years, since freshman year of high school."

The cop made a noise, not quite an agreement or a disagreement, and he put his notebook back in his pocket. I rubbed my hands on the knees of my scrubs. There were dull, dark smears where my palms were sweating.

. . .

When I walked back out the way I came, all the other nurses were staring at me openly. Even Sandy was there and I could just picture her talking to the rest of those clucking hens, telling them all about how she knew there was something wrong with me.

Even if I could somehow come back from this, I was never gonna make it work here now. Suddenly, my future which had been so clear and straightforward just a few days ago seemed like an impenetrable fog. The idea of having to retreat, to go back home and face my siblings and *her*—my stepmother—was unbearable. I even felt a strange tightness in my throat, like the very concept was causing an allergic reaction.

Outside, I turned my phone back on to see

if I'd gotten any calls. There was just one, and a voicemail. I never did get around to responding to Deborah's email so I wasn't completely surprised— talked a big game about wanting me to leave her alone and never see her again but, if I didn't contact her, she'd reach right out to draw me back in.

"Did you send the cops to my house, Everett?" She didn't even bother to say "hello." "Why would you do that? What do you think is going to happen?" She huffed a big sigh into the phone. "This is sick, Everett. You need to talk to someone because you're not okay." And then she hung up without saying goodbye.

Well, that was fucking typical Deborah. Take a situation that is incredibly difficult and dangerous for me and make it all about her. Of course I didn't send the cops to her house. Why would I do that? That's crazy-person shit. Either she thought I was some supernatural bogeyman with the power to control the LAPD or she was trying to goad me into going over to her house.

I didn't want to give her the satisfaction of knowing her dumb little trick worked but I also couldn't help but worry about what she'd been telling the cops. She was always turning people against me— our friends, her parents, even random strangers. I was sure that she'd have no problems telling the cops all about how "controlling" and "obsessive" I was.

When I drove by her apartment, I could clearly see her car parked in the lot but she must have been watching for me because, by the time I got to the door, she had all the lights off like she wasn't home. I knew she was in there, though. I could hear the little rustling sound she made when I pressed my ear flat against the door.

She was probably standing right there, two inches of shitty pressed particle board between us. She was probably doing everything she could to stifle her laughter.

That image, her standing in the dark with her hand pressed as hard as she could manage against her mouth, eyes dancing because my misfortune was just *so fucking funny*, was enough to make me want to put a brick through her window. It was only the knowledge that the police were probably watching me that allowed me to step away from her door and head back for my car.

I looked back at her place before I turned the ignition and I thought I saw something move inside.

*   *   *

Fourteen more calls from Lucy by the next morning. Nineteen e-mails and half of them had subject lines like "CALL ME PLEASE." I had to completely empty my voicemail inbox because she had filled it up.

I almost missed the cop's call because it came from an unfamiliar number and I already knew that Lucy would use other phones if she had to. I got a brusque voicemail: "This is Officer Davidson," he said, like I was supposed to know who that was, and left a number to call him back.

He answered on the second ring, like he'd been holding his phone in his hand, waiting for my call. "Mr. Priest, I wanted to ask you some questions. Is now a good time?"

"Sure." He sounded like he didn't actually care very much what kind of time it was for me.

"Have you had any contact with Julien Fraye since yesterday?"

I had been expecting to hear something about Lucy or even Deborah. "Uh . . . no. I haven't seen Ju—Mrs. Fraye since the day her husband passed away."

"And she has not contacted you in any way? Email? Phone calls?"

"No." Of all the people in the hospital, I was probably the last person that Julien would try to contact.

"And did you ever confront her with any of your suspicions about the death of Benji Fraye?"

I shook my head dumbly before remembering

that I was on the phone. "No, I barely interacted with her, honestly."

Officer Davidson was silent for so long that I asked if he was still there. "Yeah," he said, sounding both annoyed and distracted. "If she does contact you, I want you to notify me immediately, please."

I thought it was profoundly unlikely that Julien Fraye was going to call me up for a chat, but I agreed all the same. "Sir, can I ask what this is about, though?"

"You can ask," he snapped, "but it's not anything you need to know about. Just keep us posted, okay?"

"Of course," I said. After all, I was a law-abiding citizen who would do whatever he could to help the police in their investigations. After I hung up the phone, I mused on what Davidson had just told me—or strategically *not* told me. If he could get in touch with Julien, then he would have been asking her these questions instead of me. That meant she wasn't where she was supposed to be and, if he wasn't suspicious of her before, he had to be now.

My guess was that, somehow, Julien had gotten wind of what was going down with Benji and the tests I'd ordered and had blown town. She was showing herself now for what she was—a craven murderer who cared only about herself.

It would be good, of course—great even—if everyone saw how Julien had played them and how I had been right all along, but it wouldn't be nearly as satisfying if I knew that Julien was still out there with whatever she'd managed to grift from Benji and the other Frayes. It wasn't right; it worried me like grit in an oyster when women like that just got away with their bullshit because they were hot or because they played dumb or because someone in power handled them with kid gloves.

Maybe the LAPD weren't the best folks to handle this particular problem. After all, I had a few important things that they lacked: I had Emily Freeport and Allison Harper and Deepwell, Indiana. It was all just a short thirty-three hour drive away.

7

Inkweed

All parts of the plant are poisonous, causing seizures, muscles spasms and hemorrhagic diarrhea. Nevertheless, thrice-boiled inkweed leaves are a part of many culinary traditions.

The baby liked me, but that's not surprising. Babies are very visual; they like pretty things.

She liked it when I toted her around, bumping her on my hip and singing the scattered choruses of top-twenty radio hits. Joanie was grateful that I could look after her so well. At first she was a little wary, looking at me like I was going to drop the baby on its head or something, but after she saw that I could manage, she started just going about her morning routine—showering, putting on her Taco

Bell uniform, scraping together change for the bus. She should have just gotten a bus pass (or, better yet, an actual car) but I bet she never had the money for that all at one time.

Albertine still didn't think much of me and she was too young to be shy about it. She sat at the kitchen bar eating a frozen waffle and watched every move I made the way a rich woman might lurk over her housekeeper's shoulder.

"What are you going to do in school today?" I asked, trying to get something out of her other than a pout. She just shrugged her shoulders and pushed pieces of her waffle around her plate sullenly.

"Finish your breakfast!" Joan called from the bedroom. It was like she had some extra mom-sense that told her when her kids were dragging their feet.

Albertine dutifully gulped down a bite of waffle.

"Do you want something to drink?"

She just shook her head again.

"It's pay-day week," she said. I remembered pay-day week from my earliest childhood, before

Daddy quit his job altogether. Pay-day week was when you held on with all ten fingers and your nails as well because there weren't any groceries until the paycheck cleared. It was a week of peanut butter sandwiches made with just a scrape of peanut butter and one piece of bread folded over. Albertine probably knew, like I did then, that there was nothing to drink but water and there wouldn't be for a few more days yet.

It felt like the kid's version of Mardi Gras when pay-day week was finally over. Cereal, powdered drink mix, meat and boxed pasta; it was decadent, almost overwhelming.

I guess it was good that Joanie was keeping the family traditions alive.

She emerged from the bathroom in a pair of black slacks that made her hips look lumpy and a brown uniform shirt. She was wearing thick-soled black shoes, the toes peppered with grease spots. When she came to me and took Miranda from my arms, I could smell the fryer odor, though I was sure that she'd probably just washed her clothes.

"Are you taking the bus with me?" she asked. She had been annoyed to find out that I didn't intend to be her live-in babysitter and, in fact, had some things of my own to do in town.

"No." Joanie could get her own kids to daycare and school respectively, she did it every other day without me. Besides, I wanted to get to the library as soon as it opened.

"Well, just remember that I'll be home from four to five-thirty and then I'm leaving again, so make sure you're back by then." It was the third time she had given me this information. I guess once you have a kid or two, it's hard to turn off the momming.

Albertine clambered down from the kitchen stool and retrieved her purple plastic backpack from beside the door. She went over to her mother and threaded her little hand through Joanie's bigger one and she looked up at me, distrust written all over her elfin face.

"Bye," I said pointedly and didn't get even a fake little half-smile from her.

"Bye," Joanie said, like I was talking to her. She kissed me on the cheek and I waved at the baby, who opened and closed both of her fists in return.

"You can't play with my Barbies," Albertine felt the need to call over her shoulder. "You can't touch them."

* * *

I was kinda surprised that the library still had microfiche and a machine to view it on, but I suppose it made sense. The branch library nearest to Joan's house was, like the neighborhood around it, poor and underserved. There were only twelve upright shelves of books in the adult section and this weird blood-red carpet that looked like it had been ripped out of an old cinema.

The library aide (a bored teenager with a Monroe piercing right next to a huge pimple) showed me the microfiche machine in the back of the library and left me to my own devices, which was just fine for me. I flicked rapidly through the local papers, digging back about twenty years and moving to the obituaries.

It was in a library a lot like this that I had first learned that I didn't *have* to be me, if I didn't want to.

I had found the book by accident. It was mis-shelved amongst the books about how to prepare for job interviews. It was thinner than the others, almost a pamphlet, and the only thing on the cover was the title in big, bold lettering: "How to Vanish." The author was listed as "A Citizen." It told in patient detail how to find an orphaned name and take it for your own, throwing it over yourself like a big winter coat.

I read the whole thing, standing right there in the self-help section and, when I was done, I flipped to the back of the book and tore off the part of the back cover that had the library's barcode sticker printed on it. I tucked the book into my backpack and took it home where I pored over it until I had memorized every tip, every trick, every step.

Then, long after my first husband—my real first husband, not Jakob—was asleep, I used the one working stove-burner to catch it alight and then I dropped it into the sink where it could safely burn down to ash. If he had seen something like that in "his" house (which was an RV he parked on his sister's property) he'd have known right away that I was planning on leaving him.

He had seemed like a good bet at first—a man with a job who always had money to throw around. Soon, though, I found out that his primary "job" was re-selling the Vicodin he had scammed from his doctor. After three years, I figured I'd gotten just about everything I could out of him.

The appeal of "How to Vanish" wasn't in getting away from my husband, it was in scrubbing him from my life entirely—stepping out of the life where I was the child-bride of a hillbilly pill-pusher and into something else, something new and unblemished.

The book warned against using a name that I could be linked to in any way, but I thought it was the best of bad options. Emily Cherie Freeport died when she was thirteen years old in a group home, a sort of holding tank where kids without families waited for the state to get its shit together and find them a place to live. She had been born somewhere in the south (Tennessee, I eventually found out) but the group home was in Illinois. Her mom was doing thirteen years for possession and distribution, her dad was a ghost, probably long dead. She didn't even have foster parents. She was perfect.

From there, it was easy, just as the book said it would be. I sent a letter to the Secretary of State in Barnett County, Tennessee, requesting a replacement birth certificate for Emily and, without any fanfare, they sent one to me. Once I had that, getting a driver's license and other forms of ID was a peach. A few months later, I started the process of legally changing "my" name to add another layer of confusion. I wanted something that sounded classy, something that sounded right for the kind of world I wanted to live in. Julien sounded like the name of a woman on television.

It had worked well for me for five years now and I was confident that I could do it all again. The only problem was I was running out of convenient dead folks.

Two female children died in February and then none until May. One more in November, but none of the names seemed right to me. I had been very comfortable with Emily Freeport. I felt sure that she would not let me down. But these people . . . they were strangers. I had to trust that their surviving family wouldn't notice anything irregular and that the offices that issued their birth and death certificates were just busy enough or lazy enough not to notice that a dead girl was asking for her documentation.

I'd have to come back and do some more research before I made my decision, plus I had to get out of the library early to make sure that I got back to the apartment in time to catch Joan before she went to her second job.

On the way back to the bus stop, I found my eye being drawn to a small piece of abandoned land, sandwiched between two different brick buildings. It was mostly full of weeds, but I spotted a small, scrappy rosebush growing wild and what looked like a patch of yellow bindweed.

I couldn't seem to help myself, drifting over there to get a closer look. It was bindweed alright, and flowering too. Mommie showed me the tall, dull yellow shoots when I was about Albertine's age. "Never, ever eat it raw," she said, but she cooked it up for stomach complaints and monthly cramps. Mommie didn't believe in throwing any-thing away—not our old clothes, not our leftover food, not even our bathwater so, whenever we saw yellow bindweed, she would always take a cutting. Every time she did that, she would tell me the same thing—"You never know what you're gonna need in this life."

·   ·   ·

"Are you going to be here all night?" Joanie asked me as soon as I got in the door.

"I guess." What else was I supposed to do?

"Good. You can save me on a babysitter." She had changed her clothes again, or her shirt at least. This time, she was wearing a green uniform top and she had a plastic name tag pinned over her heart. Albertine was sitting in front of the TV picking at a plate of saltines with butter spread on top.

"There's Ramen noodles in the cupboard. And give them both their baths." Joanie frowned at me like she was suddenly worried about my ability to look after the girls. Kids weren't hard, though: keep them fed, keep them clean, pretty straight forward.

Still, Joanie hesitated going out the door and kept looking at us.

"It's gonna be fine," I smiled at her. "I'll take good care of them."

And I meant to, I really did mean to. But Albertine was such a spiteful little shit. Every time I told her to do something, she just sat there like she was deaf. When I asked her why she didn't do as I said, she just sneered at me. It was weird, seeing that look on a little kid's face. Unnatural.

She even tried to keep me from tending to Miranda, though the baby kept reaching out for me and making those little baby squawks and whines. Albertine was like a territorial dog, sweeping the baby up awkwardly whenever I went for her and turning her back to me.

"Albertine," I said, "I have to give Miranda a bath." She had somehow gotten something blue and sticky on her chin and it had dripped down her neck and saturated her shirtfront. Now, all sorts of dirt and bits and pieces of things were sticking to her and she was starting to look lightly furred, like she was trying to grow a beard.

"I can do it," Albertine insisted, against all evidence to the contrary.

I wasn't sure exactly what to do in this situation. It hadn't occurred to me that either of the girls would resist basic, everyday things like bathing and I did not know how to get her to do what I wanted. I didn't want to get physical with her—Joanie would throw a shit-fit if she found out about that and Albertine would just hate me all the more. I could bribe her, I supposed, but I didn't have anything she wanted.

"Okay, you can give her a bath. But how about we have dinner first?"

She still had that stubborn, hateful look on her face, but she didn't immediately object, so I took that for a good sign. "Your mom says there's some noodles in the cupboard. You like chicken or beef?"

"Chicken," she said, as begrudging as a five-year-old could sound. I found the packs of noodles right where Joan said they would be. They were practically the only thing in the cupboard, but I had something that I thought might add a little *je ne sais quoi* to the meal.

I didn't give her much, not much at all. Just a single leaf and a little bit of the stem. I dropped them into the boiling water and fished them out before putting in the flat brick of noodles. Albertine didn't appear to notice anything unusual about the soup, either. Her only complaint was that her mom usually crushed up the dried noodles into smaller pieces before steeping them in the water.

"I'll remember that for next time," I assured her.

I estimated Albertine was around thirty-five or forty pounds and so I figured she'd be feeling the effects of the bindweed pretty quickly. I was right; she hadn't even finished her noodles when she started complaining that she was too full, her belly hurt.

"Why don't you lay down in Mama's bed?" I asked, and Albertine was too exhausted to fight me on it. Her little face was all twisted up with pain and she even let me scoop her up and carry her.

I tucked her in tightly, I even filled up an old two-liter bottle with hot water and, after wrapping it in a towel, pressed it against her belly. Pretty soon, she'd start getting the shits and I figured she'd just about have it out of her system by morning.

Sickness took the bitterness out of her. She was so grateful in that moment for any kind hands that she didn't even remember that she hated me. She let me kiss her forehead, already beaded up with sweat.

Looking at her, I remembered my own childhood illnesses, when I would be exempt from chores and, at least for a day or two, Mommie would be all mine. She would make up tonics for me to drink and hot plasters for me to put on my chest. She would boil up water and fill the tub, sinking in with me in her arms until the heat and dampness loosened whatever had gotten stuck in my chest. She never scolded or looked mean at me.

Albertine would remember this time in just the same way. The time she got sick when she was little and her glamorous, worldly aunt stopped everything she was doing to take care of her. She would remember what it felt like to have all of someone's attention. To be *really* loved.

* * *

Joan had fucked up a lot as a mom.

If she was being perfectly honest with herself, her first big mistake was letting Devon get her pregnant in the first place. She'd had the occasional cigarette while she was pregnant and, in the case of Miranda, she'd been drinking pretty heavily for the first two months (though, in her defense, she didn't know she was pregnant at the time). Once, she had left Albertine sitting in a cart at a Wal-Mart and had to run all the way back from the bus stop to get her.

There had been times when the urge to hit one or both of them had been so intense that she had to lock herself in the bathroom until she calmed down.

But never before had she felt like more of a failure than when she realized what her sister had done to Albertine.

Ever since they were small, there had been something different about Julien. It was like she wasn't born with a full complement of human feelings and, instead, had to practice and practice them until she got them right. She was always watching Joan and their other siblings carefully, paying keen attention when they fell down and burst into tears or launched themselves at Mommie, overwhelmed by love. There was something puzzled and hungry in that watching, as though Julien was pressing her nose up against the glass of a room she could never figure out how to enter.

She'd gotten much better at seeming normal, at having the kind of reactions that ordinary people had and Joan had convinced herself that maybe her little sister was growing up. It was clear now, though, that she'd just had a lot more practice at faking it.

She had the nerve to try to tell Joan that she wasn't trying to hurt Albertine, that she would never hurt her niece.

"She can't get off the toilet and her temperature is one-oh-one," Joan shouted. "What is that to you? That isn't *hurting*?"

Julien looked so honestly confused. Her eyes were all big and bewildered, her cheeks and her neck had the same red flush she used to get when she was little and their parents had caught her in some sort of disobedience.

"She'll be fine," Julien insisted shrilly. "It's no worse than the stomach flu."

"How much did you give her?" Joan was crying and she hated that she was crying. They were tears of rage but she knew what they would look like to Julien—like weakness.

"I know what I'm doing," Julien scoffed,

offended that Joan would dare to question her judgement. "She'll be fine by tomorrow."

The worst part was, Joan thought she was probably right. Or, at least Joan would have to proceed as though she were right. When she had seen Albertine hunched miserably over the toilet, her little face red with fever and with fear, Joan's first instinct had been to scoop her up and take her to the emergency room, but then she remembered how much an emergency room visit cost, how much an ambulance cost, medication, doctor consultations, and Joan didn't have insurance to cover any of it. A distant (though not distant enough for Joan) second worry was how she would explain this to the doctors. If she told them what Julien had done—what her sister had done—they'd come for Julien and take her away.

It was bitter, bitter as the bindweed leaves, the idea that anything in Joan might still want to protect her sister but she did all the same. It was Julien and those two little girls, the only family she had left.

"Remember how Daddy told us family was the most important thing in the world?" Joan demanded. "That family are the only people who have any obligation to help you and protect you? He told us to take care of each other!"

That admonishment was why Joan took Julien in—why she always took her in, even though she usually wound up sneaking out in the middle of the night and taking all of Joan's cash with her. Even though she always had a long tail of trouble lashing behind her, and even though that trouble was usually one hundred percent brought upon herself. Because family was different and special and they were the ones who really *knew* you.

But Joan could see now that Julien didn't think that way at all. For Julien, her only sister and her only nieces were just more *things* that she could move around at her whim, manipulating them to get whatever she needed.

"I just wanted to make her like me," Julien sounded pitiful and not much older than Albertine herself. Julien was crying now too and Joan didn't know if they were angry tears or sad tears or crocodile tears but she didn't care anymore.

"Get out of my house," Joan said. "Never come back."

8

Lords and Ladies

Named for its resemblance to male and female genitalia, the plant features large, bright red berries which, when consumed, irritate, swell, and burn tissue in the mouth and throat.

The "road" was deeply rutted and I bounced along, jerking and careening even at less than ten miles an hour. Overhead, trees made a kind of tunnel which finally petered out into what looked like farmland. Finally, I saw a modest blue house that appeared to have once been a barn. There was an enormous pickup truck parked in front as well as a Ford Taurus and two children's bicycles, abandoned on their sides in the grass.

Other than the vehicles, there was no sign of life around the place.

When I knocked on the door, it took a couple of minutes for anyone inside to move. Through the screen door, I could see a skinny shadow peeking out of a doorway way down the front hall. It wasn't the shadow who came to the door, though, but a tiny old woman that I recognized immediately from the newspaper article. She seemed to have reached that magical age where women just sort of freeze, looking exactly the same right now as she had in a picture taken years before.

In person, though, her expression was a lot harder and sharper than in the picture. She had light blue eyes and it was remarkable how suspicious they were. "Yes?" she said. The simple greeting sounded like a curse word.

"Hi, is this the Olson farm?"

She nodded.

"And you're Loretta Olson?"

Another tight nod.

"Hi, I'm Everett Priest. I'm looking for someone I think you might know. Allison Hunt?"

Apprehension flooded her face, chasing away all that fierceness. "She's not here," the old woman said immediately. "We haven't seen her in years."

I wondered if that was really true—and if she would have told me, a total stranger, if it wasn't. Most parents (or foster parents) would be willing to cover for their children. Especially if those children fed them a steady diet of lies the way I was sure Julien had done.

"She's gone missing."

The old woman's face didn't change at all. "She's not here," she said again.

"And you don't have any idea where she might have gone?"

"To hell, I suppose," the woman scowled and I realized that I had her wrong. She wasn't trying to protect Julien, she was trying to have nothing at all to do with her.

I lowered my voice. "Honestly? I'm here because

I think that Julien did something really bad and I need to find her before she disappears completely."

After a long silence, the old woman just sighed and backed away from the door. I supposed that was all the invitation I would ever get.

．　．　．

The old man from the photo now looked more like one of those weird Incan mummies than a living man, all shriveled and curled with his skin like thin, yellow leather, and wisps of white hair. He had been propped up in a partially-reclined armchair with several heavy comforters draped over him.

"Sit," Loretta said, gesturing toward a dusty-looking loveseat. I could hear something moving around in the distant hallways, like an overgrown squirrel or rat, but I couldn't see anyone, not even the shadow I had glimpsed earlier.

"We've been taking in children to foster since 1973, when I found out I was barren," the old woman said. *Barren*, like she was some count's unsatisfactory bride in a costume drama. "Most of them came and went, a few stayed on. We taught them the value of hard work and about the Word."

Neither of those seemed like things that would be of particular interest to Julien.

"Allison came us in 1995. She was the twenty-fourth child we fostered. After she left, we never took in another. We couldn't." For the first time, her eyes flicked toward the old man in the chair. We were all silent for a moment and I realized that I could hear the old man breathing wetly, the sound a croupy baby might make.

"She . . . she did that to him?"

The old woman nodded. "Would have done worse—tried to do worse—but I caught her." She puffed up a little bit at this. "We threw her out on her ear, but the damage was done."

The damage was sitting right in front of me, staring deeply at nothing in particular.

"And you have no idea where she went?" I knew

better than to ask why the hell they hadn't notified the police. Probably some stupid notion about how people handled justice out here in the "country."

"You know, we had some bad eggs over the years. These kids, you can't imagine the lives they had nor the stock they came from. We always came down hard on them if we saw any drugs, any physical stuff." She said "physical stuff" the way someone else might say "flagrant bestiality." "But we never saw anything like Allison before. She didn't cuss or go into rages, didn't try to sneak liquor or bully the young ones. We might never have known if we didn't spot the pattern, the family always taking so ill when she had a hand in the cooking . . . " The old woman shook her head, horrifying herself at the might-have-beens. "Even when we told her to leave . . . she tried to hug me, started crying. Said this was her home."

"Didn't she have some kind of social worker or something assigned to her? Couldn't you just . . . send her back?"

"We always had the feeling that the state didn't want nothing to do with her either. We only saw her caseworker once, that first day she dropped her off. They wouldn't tell us anything about her, nothing about her parents or her upbringing. Allison wasn't even her real name, I don't think."

Jesus Christ, how many identities did Julien have?

"What kind of raising makes someone like that?" The old woman didn't seem to really be talking to me anymore so much as she was musing aloud.

"She was fourteen when we sent her away." The old woman's weird, bright eyes fixed back on me again. "We figured she was old enough to take care of herself."

"And you never heard from her again?"

The old woman hesitated. "We used to have a tradition in the house. A Christmas tradition. Each year, we would let the kids pick out a new ornament to hang on the tree. A few years ago . . ."

She trailed off and stood up, vanishing back into

the gloomy hallway outside the room without even a cursory explanation. I waited, because what else could I do? And I heard the creaking of her climbing a staircase somewhere I couldn't see. There was another sound, the low whine of a floorboard, and I looked over at the doorway in time to see a slash of pale skin and a flicker of dark hair as someone darted out of my line of sight.

A couple of minutes later, the old woman appeared with a small stack of brown cardboard boxes. "These started coming in the mail about three years ago. Return address was just a P.O. Box and there was no note, no nothing."

She passed the boxes over and I pried one open to expose a fussy-looking tear drop shaped Christmas ornament. It had that stupid-expensive look, like the kind of thing that rich people loved wasting their money on.

"But you think Allison sent these?" They were certainly tacky enough to have been from her but it seemed like a weirdly sentimental gesture for someone who had coldly poisoned her defenseless husband.

"We stopped putting up Christmas trees around the same time we turned Allison out. Without Robert's help . . . " she trailed off again, looking at the man in the chair with something that was at least in the same zip code as tenderness. "It's harder," she said finally. "Everything is."

* * *

The girl scared the shit out of me when I got out to my car and she appeared, rising up from behind the back bumper like one of those long-haired ghosts in a Japanese horror movie. "Fuck!" I said, stumbling back and steadying myself with one hand against the car.

The girl looked over my shoulder nervously at the house as though waiting for someone to appear. "You're looking for Allison?" she half-whispered.

The girl looked like a teenager, but a small and

skinny one. If you had told me she was thirteen, I'd believe you, but I'd also believe twenty-two. She had an unnatural pallor, like someone's crazy first wife who'd spent the last ten years in an attic, and one of her arms was weird. It was much thinner than the other and sort of crooked, the hand useless and flopping.

"Yeah," I said. "You know where she is?"

"You checked her husband's place?"

"Her husband is dead." Both of them, apparently, from what I'd found in Julien Hammersmith's information.

The girl scoffed. "No he's not. Trust me, I'd know if Mike Albertson kicked it."

Mike Albertson, that was a new one. "When was she married to him?"

"She moved in with him when Loretta kicked her out," the girl said. I took note of her use of "Loretta." I figured this girl was another foster kid, one of the ones who had "stuck." "Loretta was happy to see her go. Said she'd be Mike's problem."

So the old woman had been bullshitting me, though probably not to protect Julien. She probably thought that I (and the state) would take a dim view of her "giving" a minor child over to her boyfriend.

"And where does this Mike live?"

"Two towns over. Sailor's Point."

I peered at her more closely. She wore her hair thick and lank over the sides of her face, almost obscuring her eyes. "Why are you telling me?"

She shrugged and looked uncomfortable. "She's not . . . right. Allison. She was never right." It happened so quickly that I almost didn't notice, but her eyes moved to her own withered arm and then back to me.

"Thanks," I told her. "You're doing the right thing."

•　•　•

Unlike his erstwhile wife, Michael Albertson was extremely findable. It seemed that everyone in the map-dot called Sailor's Point knew who he was and where he'd be—specifically in a non-functioning RV on the back end of his sister's twenty-five acre property. The road—a path cut out by a four-wheeler—wasn't wide enough for my rental car, so I had to walk. The air was motionless and thick enough to stand a spoon up in and, by the time I reached the RV, I had sweat a dark T into the back of my dress shirt.

The sun was setting but there were no lights on in the RV. The wheels half-sunk into the soft earth and weeds had grown halfway up the walls of the vehicle. All of this squared with what I had heard in town—Michael was a perpetual loser who had moved into the RV straight out of high school and never left. His one accomplishment in life was bagging a girl as good-looking as Julien, and he'd only managed that by jumping on her when she was young and dumb.

The man himself was sitting outside the RV's open door and I wondered if he had somehow heard that I was coming to see him. Word had a way of getting around fast in little shithole towns.

"Hey there!" I called out, and the way he jerked in his plastic lawn chair told me he had not, in fact, been expecting me. He looked over his shoulder at me, his face shadowed by the brim of a camo-patterned baseball cap.

"Who the fuck are you?" He was drinking what appeared to be a wine cooler and, from the look of his slightly stumbling gait, it wasn't the first of the night.

"Everett Priest," I said, not that it could possibly have meant anything to him. "I'm looking for Ju— Allison Hunt."

Michael sighed and walked back into the RV. The metal steps gave a mournful creak as he climbed them. "You want a drink?" he called out to me. "All I got is these goddamned wine coolers, though. Payday's next week."

What job could you possibly have? I wondered.

What I actually said was, "Sure."

"Power's on the fritz." He emerged from the RV with three wine coolers trapped between his fingers. "Otherwise I'd invite you in. Turn on the AC."

"It's no problem," I said, though only an idiot would have believed anyone could be comfortable out there where the air was like a down comforter soaked in soup.

"Well? Pull up a seat." Michael gestured lazily at a pile of folded lawn chairs leaned up against the RV. I took one and unfolded it with a rusty whine.

Up close, I could see that Michael was not a bad-looking man. He was starting to bloat up a little bit (his wine cooler habit probably had something to do with that) and he had a weak chin, but he could probably cover that up with a beard. I could see why, as a fourteen-year-old itching to get away from home, Julien might have imagined that he was some kind of Prince Charming.

"So"—he cracked the top on a wine cooler (Strawberry Sensation) and passed it to me—"you're chasing after Ally, huh? What'd she do? Rob you? Cheat on you?"

As if I would ever be taken in by a transparent grifter like Julien. "Something . . . a little more serious than that."

Michael nodded sagely. "Yeah, I figured she'd get into some real shit one of these days."

"Real shit?"

"That kid was crazy. Is still crazy, I guess. Run off in the middle of the night, no note, no nothing. Could have been dead in a ditch for all I knew."

Somehow, I had a feeling he hadn't exactly been out scouring the ditches. "Yeah she's pretty . . . out there."

"You think that's the fun of it at first, you know? Crazy and hot, you think it's just gonna be some weird sex, but then she's trying to light your house on fire with a curling iron and putting Drano in your cereal and you wonder when it all became a *relationship*."

Besides being possibly the most disheartening

description of a relationship I'd ever heard, that bit about the Drano sounded promising. "She tried to poison you?"

Michael laughed like he was telling me some wacky story about his wild youth. "*Try*, shit, she succeeded! I just didn't die." He took a long drink from his wine cooler. "It takes a lot to kill an Albertson. You know I once broke my arm deer hunting, spent the whole night in the woods at about six degrees and I was totally fine. Didn't even get frostbite."

I could think of few things I cared less about but I forced myself to look interested. "But the Drano thing . . . ?"

"Oh, I don't know if it was actually Drano, but whatever it was, it sure tore my guts up. It was coming out of both ends like a goddamned firehose, if you know what I mean. That was her little way of letting me know that she knew about a girl I was talking to."

Charming.

"I mean, I'm not saying I'm a saint. I messed around, she messed around, we fought a lot. We were young and dumb."

According to my research in town, he had been nearly twenty when they got together, compared to Julien's fourteen. "Dumb," I could buy but "young" was relative.

"And her folks tried to tell me how she was. Hard to handle."

The sort of "hard to handle" that might lead a family to essentially sign their young daughter over to a grown man who lived in a defunct RV, I guessed. If it was possible to feel any sort of pity for Julien Fraye, I would be feeling it now.

"They told you about the . . . the poisoning?"

Michael shrugged. "I never *saw* her do anything. When I started barfing up my innards, she pretended she didn't have nothing to do with it. She even tried to tell me that I probably had food poisoning!"

That was practically the same story she tried

with Benji. I was willing to bet that she had used the same poison in all these cases, too. Everywhere she went, Julien left a trail of sick and dying people. Was everyone around her really so taken in by her dingbat charms that they couldn't see what was right in front of them?

"I suppose you're waiting for her too?" Michael asked, disrupting my silent musings.

"Waiting?"

"She called about four hours ago. Said she was coming home."

He had to be paraphrasing. I could not imagine Julien ever referring to this place as "home." "Yeah," I said, "I'm waiting for her. If that's alright with you."

Michael gave me a lazy shrug and stared off toward the woods at the edge of his sister's property. "No skin off my nose," he said.

* * *

"So, you'd take her in, then?" I asked eventually, two and a half wine coolers making me a lot less comfortable with silence. "After everything she did?"

Michael laughed, chin tucked into his chest like someone had just whispered a joke into his ear. "You know what that girl was? She was what my daddy would have called a *pistol.*"

My "daddy" would have called her something different. "Wife Number Four," probably. I was so thankful I hadn't inherited that particular strain of stupid.

"On our third date, we robbed a gas station," Michael continued. "Got seven hundred dollars and didn't make it out of the damn parking lot. Somehow, she managed to get the charges dropped against her. I did three months in county lockup. Bitch." He said the word fondly, almost nostalgically. In a sad sort of way, it must have been the best time in his life, running with a beautiful and volatile woman and fooling himself into thinking the two of them might have some sort of grand future in petty crime.

"Soon as I got out, I went looking for her." He tipped his wine cooler at me. "Just like you."

Hardly the same situation.

"I found her at her foster parents' place, wearing them long skirts like she was going to sing in the church choir, and she just looked at me with them big green eyes and I couldn't figure out how to hate her."

I was reminded of how my father used to rage about my stepmother when she would leave for hours on end, conveniently "forgetting" to charge her phone. He always said it was the last time, that he wasn't going to be made a fool. But then she would crawl into his bed at three, four, five in the morning smelling like cigarettes she didn't smoke and she'd do what she did best and, by morning, he was whistling while he made her a goddamned smoothie.

Some men were just made of weaker stuff.

"That was when she first told me her whole sob story," Michael slurred conversationally. "About her parents—her real parents. Dunno how much was true, but I believed it when she said it."

"What happened to her real parents?" The old woman had said that Child Services seemed happy to get rid of Julien, that they'd given her a new name for a new life. That was not, in my experience, standard foster care procedure.

"The federal fucking government happened to them!" Michael crowed. "Uncle Sam! Put 'em down like they was fuckin' Al Qaeda. It was the nineties, suppose we didn't have as much to worry about then. Government could spend more time sniffing around ordinary citizens who just happened to be a little . . . different."

" . . . different?"

Michael waved one hand through the air, shooing away the mosquitos. "Her mother was an old-fashioned-type preacher. Hellfire, end-times, demons and shit."

That didn't sound so unusual, especially for this part of the world. If I had to live in rural Indiana, I'd probably start looking forward to a fiery apocalypse as well.

"Whatever she was selling, though, I guess people were buying. They started up a little community sort of thing not too far from here, actually. In the hills out by the state forest. Had ten or fifteen families up there, I believe. Then a couple of people wound up dying and Ally's dad got busted on some old assault charge. They found a few guns when they searched his truck and it all went to shit from there—"

"Wait, wait—people *died*? How?"

"Ally didn't say much about that. She was just a little thing when this all went down but, from what I gather, her mom was doing these kinds of services, rituals, I guess you'd say, where she tested people's faith. Some folks weren't faithful enough, apparently. Though, to my mind, you can't really say she *killed them* if they drank the poison of their own free will."

"Allison's mother poisoned people too?"

Michael laughed. "I don't think that's how she would have described it. But yeah, how else did you think Ally came by it?"

Since I'd met her, I'd presumed that Julien had some sort of unhappiness in her past but I was expecting something more mundane, like a Touchy Uncle. This was some next level shit.

"So what happened when the feds went up there?"

"Siege. They held out a few days, too. By then, most of the other families had left or been driven out. It was just Ally and her family. Ally was the only one come out alive." He scratched his belly thoughtfully. "Actually, there may have been two of them. I think she mentioned a sister once."

"Holy shit."

"Yup."

I finished the rest of my wine cooler in one gulp and tossed the bottle into the tall grass.

* * *

Julien came up the road on foot, just like I had. She had her high heels in one hand and there were small, half-moon sweat stains underneath her breasts like winking eyes.

She got almost all the way to the RV before she saw me. I saw her eyes widen just the tiniest bit and I knew that she was going to run. Sure enough, she bolted immediately for the protection of the trees. Just as fast, I was up from my seat and after her.

Julien had a good stride on her but she clearly didn't do much regular cardio because we were only halfway to the trees and she was already starting to flag. I was going to overtake her easily and that knowledge felt . . . good. It reminded me of the one and only time in my life that I had been hunting. Rabbit hunting, in particular. Once we found the den—a disordered heap of snowy branches—it was my little sister's job to shake the whole structure until the little furry things came darting out, running directionless all over the new snow.

When I got close enough, I reached out and gave her a shove between her shoulder blades. She stumbled as I'd hoped she would but recovered and tried to zig-zag away from me, but I caught her elbow and pulled her down into the grass.

She didn't say anything. At least, not anything that I could identify as human words, only grunts of frustration as she thrashed against me. She tried to crawl away from me, but I brought my fist down hard on the curve of her spine and sent her crashing face-down back into the dirt. I should have pinned her there but I didn't move fast enough and she was able to roll herself over. She became a dervish of knees and elbows underneath me, jabbing at my stomach, my groin, any place she thought might be a little bit vulnerable. She even wrapped her hands around my head and clawed deeply at my scalp. I grabbed a hank of her long yellow hair and knotted it around my fist, pulling it as hard as I could and slamming her skull repeatedly against the dry dirt beneath us. I realized that I was shouting, "Stop fighting!" over and over again.

Eventually, she did as I demanded, her whole body going still and limp, like a dead person. She stared up at me, looked right into my eyes like she was trying to burn through them. Her face was smeared with dirt and criss-crossed with little bleeding lines, like cat scratches. She didn't remind me of a rabbit anymore. Now I thought she was more like a snake, impaled on a stick but still alive, writhing and twisting and just aching for a chance to spit poison.

My heart was hurting me, pounding much harder and faster than it should have been after that brief little run. My face and my neck were tingling, like they did right after I came. I had a strange, wild urge to hit her, just with an open hand. I wanted suddenly to see the face she would make, how shocked she would be, but how helpless as well.

"What are you doing, you fucking lunatic?" she hissed at me, which I thought was pretty rich, all things considered.

"Citizen's arrest." My voice came out more ragged and higher pitched than I was expecting. Jesus, I sounded like a teenage boy caught jacking off at the family computer.

"That's not real, that's just something you saw on TV," Julien said, but I could see a little glimmer of doubt in her eyes.

"We'll find out"—I got to my feet and pulled her up with me—"when I call the cops on your murdering ass."

I twisted her arms up behind her back the way I used to do with my little sister. Long grass was caught in her hair and I had a feeling that she was thinking as hard as she could, trying to slither her way out of this one.

I pushed her all the way back to the RV where

Michael was still sitting in the same spot, working on the same wine cooler. "Michael," Julien said once, pleadingly, but he didn't even look at her.

"You got any rooms with locks on them in there?" I asked him.

"Bathroom," he grunted, pointing toward the aft end of the RV. He stared into space, trying his hardest not to be involved.

I guided Julien up the steps and into the vehicle, which smelled like B.O. and overcooked hotdogs. "This isn't any of your business, you know," Julien said, making her voice low and quiet. "You're a stranger to all these people."

I guided her through the RV, past the laminate kitchen table heaped with dirty paper plates and plastic cutlery, past a repellant collection of two-liter bottles partially full of an unknown liquid, toward a small fake-wood door, half-opened to reveal a surprisingly tidy bathroom.

I pushed her into the bathroom and, as soon as her body left my grip, she turned to look me in the face. Her lower lip was bleeding; it was split right down the middle. "What do you want?" she asked, making her bright green eyes large and yet sharp somehow. It felt like she was flaying me with her gaze, peeling back my skin and musculature, leaving me just bones. "Whatever it is, I can make it happen for you." Her voice was a murmur, a rill, the sound of a narrow creek dribbling over flat rocks.

I should have had something ready, some witty retort that I could toss off casually to let her known how little she affected me. Instead, I just shut the door on her and her weird, penetrating eyes. I turned the small lock on the doorknob and tried to shake the feeling that I had only barely escaped from something.

She started banging on the door and howling obscenities before I had even gotten out the RV's door.

· · ·

The policewoman on the phone got real pissy when I suggested that they send their most senior officer, but I couldn't risk this rinky-dink town blowing this. Julien had managed to kill two husbands on the LAPD's watch. I could only image the havoc she might wreak in Sailor's Point, Indiana.

Maybe they were stung by my insistence on a competent officer, but the local police actually showed up pretty quickly. Three officers on quads came roaring up just as the sun was setting. "You the one that called?" the first officer asked, squinting in my general direction.

I would have figured that was obvious from the stiff way Michael was holding his hands in his lap and staring straight ahead. It was pretty clear that he was not a dude who frequently summoned the police of his own volition.

"Yeah," I said, "I caught an interstate fugitive. Wanted for murder. *Multiple* murders," I added when the cop just gave me a skeptical look.

"And you are . . . ?"

"A doctor. From LA" I could only imagine the snickers that would ensure if I admitted to being a nurse. "I cared for her husband, before she killed him."

"And then you followed her clear out here?"

"Why don't you take her into custody and then figure out how I fit into all of this, huh?" I snapped and the officer just shrugged as though it made no difference to him either way. He ambled toward the trailer, his hand on his belt, though as far as I could see, he wasn't carrying.

I wasn't sure if I was supposed to follow him or wait outside, and from the awkward shuffling the other cops were doing, they weren't too sure either, so we all just waited until he called out. "Hey, doc? You wanna come back here?"

I ventured into the trailer, the other officers right on my heels like I was the professional law enforcer and they were the timid good Samaritans. I could see the lead officer as soon as I stepped inside the doorway. He was standing in front of the now-open bathroom door and he had the most disgusting expression on his face. There's nothing worse than seeing a stupid person looking smug about how smart they think they are. "Looks like your murderer up and vanished," he chuckled, gesturing toward the inside of the bathroom which was in fact empty.

9

Trailing Bittersweet

An invasive weed in the potato family. All parts of the plant are toxic to humans but usually not fatal.

We had all heard it a thousand times, the story of how Daddy met Mommie and convinced her to love him but we used to beg him to tell it again and again. He always did because, of the two of them, Daddy was the soft one. The real romantic.

Mommie grew up in a family just like ours, lots of brothers and sisters who lived on a big farm. Every so often, they would have to go into the city and, when they did, Grandpa and Grandma would pack up all the kids and have them walk in two lines, like the little orphan girls in the Madeline books.

"Most of the time," she said, "no one could tell us apart."

Maybe, then, that was what made her fall in love with Daddy, because he saw the long, gray line of them standing up on a city bus and he picked her out right away.

I'm gonna marry that girl, he thought. At least, that's how he told it.

But he was walking down the sidewalk and she was on a bus and any sensible person might have figured he was never, ever going to see her again. But my daddy was not a sensible person.

The bus was starting to pull away, leaving forever. So that's when Daddy did a lunatic thing and hurled himself right in front of it, bouncing off the wide, flat bumper like an abandoned puppet, strings cut and dangling.

"It didn't hurt," he would always say at that point in the story, "I knew how to take a hit."

The bus stopped all the same and, when Daddy got to his feet, he could see Mommie's bright face looking worried at him out the window. He locked his eyes on hers and stared her down until she broke away from the long gray line of her sisters and walked out of the bus—until she walked right into his arms.

I know why my brothers and sisters asked to hear that story again and again and again. They liked the way Daddy would toss his body around to imitate his movements and they liked the funny voice he would use for the bus driver. What I liked about it, though, was that it was a love story. It was the best love story I had ever heard. Whenever he told that story, I imagined what it would be like to be a grown up and to have someone love me like that, love me so much they'd sacrifice their body and risk everything they had.

These days, I was starting to think that no one was ever going to love me like that. Not Benji, who just wanted some living proof of his virility, or Jakob, who never valued me even half as much as his career. Not my sister who had shunned me or Michael who had betrayed me. Not the folks who promised to take me in and make me part of a family. Every single one of them had failed me and I was left with no one to take care of me, except for myself.

That was okay, though, because Mommie had shown me how.

* * *

Mommie talked a lot about death. She said it was her job to teach us all about being alive and a big part of that was dying. She told us all the many things that she would die for and all the things she would die before she saw happen. Like the government taking her kids away, or locking up her husband, or silencing her speaking of the gospel, or taking any of the other things that belonged to us by right.

Most of those things were still up there, tucked protectively into the hills. Almost all the cabins were still standing and the big garden I'd worked so many hours in was still sprouting and blooming, but badly in need of care. I started there, pulling up weeds until my long fingernails started to break off, one by one, dirt crusting underneath them.

I didn't leave the garden until I had clean rows. The potatoes and the tomatoes and the seasoning herbs, and in the last two rows, the other herbs. Mommie's herbs. I touched them each and I named them, just like Adam and the beasts.

Monkshood, jimsonweed, dumb cane, belladonna, oleander . . . I was home.

* * *

All the furnishings were gone from the cabin, save for the shelves and bedframes Daddy had built into the walls. So I slept on the soft wooden floorboards after I cleaned a place for myself with some old rags

I'd found in the remains of the kitchen sink. Once upon a time, we had a well and I figured I would fix it so I could pump up some water again.

I found a couple of blankets. They smelled musky and earthen but weren't too torn. That would do well enough for me. I wasn't the princess anymore who slept on three-thousand-dollar-a-night hotel beds. I was just little June Judge Felix, named for the work that Mommie had Seen for me.

I'd slept on this floor many times before. It was a punishment when I did something bad, getting exiled from the bed I shared with Joanie. It wasn't exactly comfortable, but it was familiar. One of the first things I did when I got to the cabin was clear out the fireplace and get a good fire going. Daddy had built that fireplace and chimney himself with rocks we took out of this dirt. In addition to the sachet of powdered crowshood, I always kept a box of matches and a small hunting knife in my purse. I had found that, between the three of them, I could solve most problems.

In the morning, I would see about setting some traps. There were small animals, varmints out in the woods, and I knew how to catch them. Most of the vegetables Mommie planted were rotting in the ground but I would dig them up and save the seeds. You never know what you might need.

· · ·

Used to be, this place was never quiet. When we were at our largest, we had eleven other families living up there with us. There was never any short-age of kids running underfoot, the men were always working, Mommie was always with the women, singing and teaching and witnessing

Even in the end, there were still shouts and screams and whispers.

Maybe that's why I've never liked being alone, because I never had to learn how when I was a kid? They split Joanie and me up almost as soon as our parents were dead and, at the group home, I used to crawl into bed with the older girls just to feel near to them. Some would let me snuggle up against them; others would squeal and push me out. It didn't matter that much to me either way. It was all noise and warmth and eyes on me.

I was almost relieved when, on the fifth day, I heard the pickup truck rumbling up the hill toward the compound.

* * *

We heard them coming that other day too. They tried to be sneaky, but Daddy and my brother Billy knew everything that happened in this forest and they could feel it when something was different, when something was wrong.

Daddy came into the cabin and told Mommie, "It's happening." She went up in the loft to the bed they shared and brought down one of the rifles. Billy already had a gun and Daddy too and Mommie produced a .22 for Joan but nothing for me—and, of course, nothing for the baby Lester who was just starting to crawl. I was much bigger than Lester but Mommie said that it was still too dangerous.

When I heard the truck coming, I thought about grabbing my knife but I decided against it. Our guns hadn't saved us, how could one modest little blade rescue me now?

I thought also about heading off into the deeper woods. What little there were in the way of roads ended right at this compound, if they wanted to follow me, they would have to go on foot and run the risk of getting hopelessly lost. But I couldn't quite bring myself to do it. It had been five days since I saw another living person and something in me went cold at the idea of pushing further into that uninhabited silence.

And so I waited and I listened and I put Mommie's old kettle on.

• • •

We waited three days for the government men to come get us. Mommie tried to distract us with stories from the bible, stories from when she was a little girl. She tried to tell the story of how she and Daddy met when Joan begged but it wasn't the same.

Mostly, she talked to us about heaven. She said we were all going there soon and that we could be sure of that because we would die righteous, steadfast in our faith no matter how much the worldly people tried to crush us.

They shot Daddy through the window. They'd been trading bullets back and forth and Mommie made all us kids lay flat on the floor. She had to press her hand down on Lester's back because he was too little to understand.

Daddy didn't die right away but I could tell it was bad because Mommie didn't even try to do anything for him, she just made that awful crying sound and held his hand. He wrapped both of his hands around hers; it looked like it was hard for him. He couldn't really talk and the bullet had made a hole in his chest that sucked and whined like the sound you hear when you drive through a tunnel real fast.

That was the second day.

That night, Mommie told us we all had to be strong, that the worldly people would try to take everything away from us, but we had to resist and we had to protect what was ours. Daddy was still in the corner underneath the window, but Mommie had taken the cloth off the table and put it over him. I wondered if he was going to start to smell. Lester's diapers smelled and we didn't dare open the door to toss them out.

I was glad, though, that Mommie let us all sleep in the big bed with her. Everyone was so close, talking in low voices, holding on to one another. I drank them up with my eyes. I wanted to absorb them through my skin. I wanted them to look at me and talk to me and cradle me forever.

• • •

I guess I was expecting the police—local boys in their county-issued SUV. It was a local boy alright, but not the law. I recognized that truck. It was the same one Michael'd always had. He used to drive me everywhere in that old bucket of rust. Mainly to places that were far away from town and got real dark at night.

It wasn't actually Michael, though. As the truck pulled up, I could see out the window that someone taller and younger was driving it. Someone with sleek dark hair—Fuckface from the hospital. I smiled, even though no one was there to see it. He'd come all this way to see me.

· · ·

The morning after Daddy died, Mommie got up early in the morning, almost before the sun rose. She let us kids keep sleeping, which was rare—if Mommie was up, everyone was up. I have always been a light sleeper though, and I watched her through slivered eyes as she moved around the kitchen, rifling in the pantry with purpose.

She came out with the flour, the sugar, the last of our big, coarse eggs, and a few bundles of herbs. She was making us pancake breakfast. My favorite. I nudged Joanie until she woke up too and pointed at Mommie's back as she took down the big mixing bowl. I was surprised to see that Joanie was frowning, because pancake breakfast was her favorite too.

"Get on up," Mommie said. Joanie was moving around too much so of course she could tell we weren't really sleeping. "And get the baby up too."

We had to move around very quietly and keep away from the windows. We crept like shadows, half-hunching down and keeping close to the floor. It was sort of fun, like a game of hide and seek.

Joanie looked after Baby Lester, I went to the kitchen to help Mommie. She had all her ingredients laid out in a neat line, the way she always did when she cooked. She cracked an egg into the bowl and in the enforced silence of the cabin, it sounded awful, like a small bone snapping.

"I don't need help here, June," she said. I wasn't good at cooking anyways. That was something Joanie did.

"Mommie," I asked her, "when will the worldy people go away?"

Mommie kept her back to me so I couldn't see how her face looked when she said, "They don't go away, little one. Not ever. Not until we shuck these bodies and join Him."

I had asked my mother once why there were so many of the worldy people and so few of us and she told me that people started to fall in love with their comforts and their earthly pleasures. They got so blinded by that love that they forgot about the promise of heaven. *I* never got distracted by loving things. I always figured that I was made just to *get* love, to pull it into me like air.

Joanie was still over by the bed, trying to figure out how to tie a towel around Lester so it would stay on and serve as a diaper. The worldy people had blocked up the well, no water in the cabin but what we had stored. Mommie had to use goat's milk—two days old and warm—for the pancakes.

Mommie had us pray before we ate, just like always. I wondered if the worldly people outside could smell the buttery sweetness of the pancakes. I wondered if they were as hungry as I was.

Joanie was holding my hand too tight and too stiff. She didn't wanna let go even when Mommie said we could start. She ate slow, tiny little bites and chewed so much that Mommie had to chide her, "Eat your food, Joan Witness Felix."

Joanie nodded and swallowed and under the table, she squeezed my knee so hard that I jolted in my seat. Mommie didn't notice that, though. She was feeding Lester, mashing the pancakes up with honey until they formed a paste that she could scoop into his mouth.

Dead-man's-breath is a shrub with little white flowers that blossom in early summer. It has a certain resemblance to baby's breath, thus the name. Its effects are immediate and intense. Within ten to twenty minutes (depending on the dosage) a victim will start to convulse violently. Most people pass out then and they just go to sleep while their respiratory system freezes inside them. If you have to kill something, Mommie once told me, dead-man's-breath is just about the kindest way to do it.

It took a little less than ten minutes for Baby Lester to stiffen up so much that he couldn't hold himself in his seat anymore. Mommie took him and laid him down on the floor real gentle. Then, she stretched out there herself and called to us. "Girls," she said, "come be with us."

Joanie spat a mouthful of pancake out, slick and brown as a slug. "June," she whispered, "stick your fingers down your throat. Do it now!" and then she did as she advised, retching right there on the floor until she brought up everything in her stomach, which wasn't too much.

I just watched her, not doing nothing.

"C'mon," I said, when she was done. I took her hand (the one that wasn't slick with saliva) and led her over to the spot on the floor. Mommie must have given the largest dose to herself, her breathing was very slow, one rasp every ten or fifteen seconds.

I laid down and pulled Joanie with me.

"June . . . " she moaned, tears in her eyes.

I petted her hair because even I could see that she needed some comfort. "It's okay," I said brightly. "We just have to do like Mommie says; we just have to be stronger than whatever is hurting us."

As usual, Mommie had the right of it.

10

Heart of Jesus

Sometimes called Elephant Ears or Angel Wings, causes burning sores in the mouth and throat sufficient to prevent speaking or breathing.

At first the local police had "strongly advised" me to stay in town. Even after I pointed out the ripped bathroom window screen and disturbed grass, I don't think they were entirely convinced I hadn't completely fabricated Julien.

Everything changed, though, with a series of irate phone calls from Officer Davidson, both to me and, apparently, the Sailor's Point Police Department. Initially, he wanted to know why I had "fled town" and when I corrected him about why I had left town in an entirely legal and reasonable manner, he said he had to check on some things and would call me back.

Two days later, local officers Glenn and Jamison knocked on my door at the Sailor's Point Roundtree Lodge to inform me that they were launching a statewide search for Julien Fraye. "Thank you for the . . . tip," Officer Glen said, sounding like someone had a gun pressed against his ribs at that very moment.

"I want to help," I said and watched both of their eyebrows shoot up at once.

"I guess he can . . . put up fliers?" Officer Jamison, clearly the younger of the two, said timidly.

"I would prefer to help with the physical search," I said before Officer Glenn could respond.

"I'm sure you would," Glenn sneered, "but that is not your job. We have set up the appropriate barricades. She's not going to get away."

. . .

My cellphone said "Dad" when it rang and I took a second to calm myself before answering. "Hi Corrin," I said as neutrally as possible.

"Hi, sweetheart," my stepmother's voice oozed out of the cell speakers, thick and cloying as honey. "How are you doing?"

"I'm fine. What's up, Corrin?" We both knew that she wouldn't contact me unless she wanted something.

"Sweetheart, we're worried about you."

She used to talk that way when Dad was alive, too, like she had melded the two of them into a single horrible organism. Now she had absorbed my younger sister.

"We had a police officer call the house looking for you. Is it true that you left your job at the hospital? You know what kind of favors I called in to get you that—"

"I didn't leave anything. It's . . . not a good fit. I'm taking some time off. A . . . vacation."

I looked around the grim, stuccoed walls of the

motel room. Sailor's Point was no one's idea of a hot getaway spot.

"I just wanted to make sure you were *well*," she said delicately and I knew exactly what she was up to. How many times in my childhood had it happened? The night before a major soccer game or debate regionals and there she'd be, touching my cheeks and forehead, telling me how I was burning, feeding me chicken and stars from the can and sitting at my bedside with that fake concerned look on her face. Instead of doing anything that might distinguish myself, anything that might take the spotlight from her for even the briefest moment, I would spend my day retching into a plastic tub.

Once, when I was seventeen, I vomited so hard that I must have roughed up my esophagus because I started producing little puddles of blood. Dad wanted to take me to the hospital but Corrin fought him. It was the first time I'd ever seen her be afraid and that's when I knew. I never ate anything she gave me after that and I left home the day after high school graduation.

When Corrin realized she couldn't sicken my body, she tried attacking my mind, telling me that I was having "obsessive thoughts," that I needed to "manage my anger." Once when I was still in nursing school she 5150'd me—had me involuntarily committed—after I kicked out her back door. She said I was "manic," but conveniently failed to mention how she'd invited me over and ambushed me with some random woman she claimed was a therapist.

"I'm fine. Feeling great." It was hard to get the words out through the grinding of my teeth.

"Oh, sweetheart, I wish you'd come home," she sighed. "It's been so hard since your father passed . . . "

I was twelve when my father married Corrin and all my friends teased me about my hot stepmom, saying how jealous they were, like I'd be the one fucking her. The hell of it was, I had a feeling that if I went back to that house, she might try just that. She was in her late forties now and she'd expected a bigger chunk of dad's estate—she'd expected a bigger estate in general. She was probably on the prowl for a new man and a new bank account to siphon.

That wasn't me, though. That would never be me.

"Listen, Corrin, I gotta go. I'm needed here."

. . .

I stopped drinking when Dad died, part of my on-going attempt to be nothing like him. Almost a year I'd made it but I'd already popped my seal out at Michael's RV and, as the two primary leisure activities in Sailor's Point appeared drinking and protracted suicide, I figured I'd better pick up a bottle of bourbon.

It wasn't very good but it was good at getting me drunk, which I appreciated in a bourbon.

I drank it warm, too lazy and eventually too wasted to go to the ice machine, and I dialed Deborah's number over and over again. When we first started dating, it was incredible. It was like I always had someone in my corner. Whenever Corrin would pull some crazy bullshit, Deborah would rage about her and assure me I was in the right. She was so good back then, before she went away to college and everything got ruined.

I realized eventually that she must have changed her number again. She first pulled that shit eight months ago but, just like God, Deborah didn't close a door without cracking a window.

It took me a few tries to punch in Deborah's sister's number and she must have saved my number because she answered me with, "I told you to stop fucking calling me. Deb's restraining order says you can't contact any immediate family members."

"Whaa? Wha the fuck?" I slurred. "I's've never been to court!"

"You didn't need to," Deborah's sister sighed.

"All she had to do was prove that you're a danger to her and she has plenty of proof of that, asshole."

I left the city for less than a week and Deborah had already snuggled up to some dumb judge, batting her eyelashes and telling a one-sided story about what a dangerous monster I was. And of course the court was falling all over itself to believe her.

I threw the mostly empty bottle of bourbon, which bounced pathetically off the ancient, crushed-down carpet. It landed on its side, dribbling brown liquid.

"Won't get my deposit back . . . " I chortled to myself, everything suddenly unbearably funny. "Won't get any of it back!"

•   •   •

The journey back to Michael's RV involved another bottle (this one of crappy beer) and a lot of long black stretches of nothingness. I wasn't even totally sure how I got out there but I surfaced from one such blank period to find myself crawling awkwardly through the back window of his pickup truck.

I shimmied in like a spastic eel and was delighted to find that Michael kept his keys in the disused ash tray. And, like any good redneck, he had a gun in the truck, a long, murderous-looking black rifle wrapped in a knit blanket.

I started the car and turned it around in the tall grass, heading down that long, impassable drive toward the road when I realized that my phone had voicemail on it. I stabbed at it with clumsy fingers—maybe Deborah was feeling mournful or spiteful or a little bit of both.

Instead, it was Mariah, using her driest, most bureaucratic voice. "Mr. Priest, I just wanted to inform you that your employment at St. Eustachius has been rescinded. We reserve the right to pursue legal action in the matter of Benjamin Fraye's medical records."

Of course you do, I thought, nestling the beer between my legs. "Kill the fucking messenger,"

I said to no one in particular. "That'll fix the problem."

• • •

I knew where to go; Michael had told me. I just had to drive up into the hills and look for an unmaintained road. "The only roads up there go to the compound," he'd said. That's where I'd find her, I figured, her first home in the world and the only one she had left.

By the time I drove all the way up there, though, I was starting to sober up and starting to wonder if what I was doing wasn't, in fact, totally bug-fuck crazy. I could barely see the "road" that I was driving on and I couldn't be completely sure that it wasn't just an extra-wide hiking path. I wasn't at all sure that I was going in the right direction or that Julien would be there even if I somehow managed to find the place.

And if she *was* there . . . well, that raised some even bigger questions.

I was still drunk enough—or just stubborn enough—to keep going until I crested one rolling hill and could see down into a little valley, less forested than the ones around it. There were what appeared to be a cluster of buildings, half-visible between the trees. It looked a little bit like those old half-preserved ghost towns you see up in gold country.

In a manner of speaking, I supposed that's just what it was. Except, in those ghost towns, none of the chimneys were letting off smoke.

· · ·

He had a gun, which also probably belonged to Michael. He was pointing it at me as soon as I stepped out of the cabin.

"Whoa!" I said, raising up my empty hands. "I'm not armed."

"I am," the nurse said, not moving. His eyes were dull and reddened, his stubble had blossomed into a proto-beard, and he was a little unsteady on his feet.

"Yeah? And what you gonna do with that gun?"

"The police are looking for you in Bloomington and Indianapolis and all over the state," he said, only slurring his words a little. "Nobody's looking up here. Because nobody knows what you are. I could shoot you in the head right now and no one would ever know."

"You think you know what I am?"

The gun barrel dipped a little and I saw it again, that scornful, superior look he'd worn in Benji's hospital room. "Of course," he spat. "You think you're smart, you think you're sly, but I saw you. I saw you the moment we met."

You did, I thought. I had run out of people to love me. I'd have to settle now for someone willing to just look at me.

"Come inside with me," I said and smiled.

"I'm not going anywhere with you."

I took an experimental step forward. He didn't move. "You came across the country for me. What's a few more steps?" We were less than a foot apart now. The barrel of his gun was hovering an inch from my chest. I wasn't afraid of him shooting me, though. I was more afraid of him getting back in that truck and driving away, leaving me to the silence.

"I'm bringing the gun," he said, lowering it slowly until he was holding it lengthwise like a log for the fire.

"My daddy woulda approved," I said teasingly, taking his elbow and guiding him toward the open cabin door.

* * *

The water in the kettle was burbling. I took it off the fire and pointed at the table, where I'd set out the two least-cracked coffee cups I found in the old cupboards. "You look like you could use a cup of coffee."

He hovered around the table but did not sit down.

"This is where your mother killed all those people?"

I rolled my eyes and pulled the kettle off the fire. All I had was instant coffee, an old can left in one of the cupboards but there was some of Mommie's honey in there too. I spooned some into both cups before pouring in the boiling water. "All those people," I snorted. "*Three*. Three people passed and they were weak. They knew it, too. Otherwise they wouldn't have been scared to be tested."

The nurse must have gotten tired of standing around, because he finally took a spot at the table, gun laid across his legs. "Is that what you were doing to your husbands? Giving them a test?"

I laughed as I set the steaming cup in front of him. "Shit, no. I knew everything I needed to about those men, no testing required. I was *killing* them."

I took my place across the table. "Drink up," I said. "It'll clear your head."

. . .

The cup in front of me was unremarkable. Black coffee, uncut with milk. It had a flowery smell from the thick, dark honey I'd watched Julien stir into it. I wrapped both hands around the cup. It was hot—almost burning—and I realized that I'd been cold all this time.

"And what about your foster family? Did you want to kill them, too?"

Julien's face hardened and her little coquettish half-smile slipped away. "They were liars," she said. "They promised to love me but they never did. They just loved feeling good about themselves, bringing in a poor, lost waif, thinking all about what good Christians they were." Julien shrugged and sipped her own coffee. "So I showed them what they really were. They didn't like what they saw."

"Your little foster sister too? She needed to be crippled, that's what you're saying?"

Julien set her coffee cup down so hard some of liquid jumped out and splashed on the table. "How was I supposed to know she'd have seizures? I'd never seen anyone react that way before and I barely gave her anything, just a pinch. There was probably something wrong with her to begin with."

She really believed that, I realized. That her poison was just drawing out the weakness in people and exposing it to the air.

"You aren't drinking your coffee," she pointed out.

I was still just holding it, my palms practically numbed from the heat.

Julien smiled at me. It was amazing, how much her smile was like the unconscious grin of a wolf or a fox—red tongue, white teeth—and how it was also one of the most lascivious things I'd ever seen a woman do. "Are you afraid?" she asked, leaning toward me so I could see down her shirt. It was the same shirt she'd been wearing when she broke out of Michael's RV, crusted with sweat, discolored by dirt. Her hair was unwashed, her feet were bare, and her legs streaked with mud. Yet somehow, she was still the most fuckable thing in the whole state.

Corrin was like that too, in her glory days. No matter how bad she looked, how little makeup she wore, there was a feral sexuality in her. Her and Julien both, it was like they ran a little hotter, shone a little brighter than the rest of the world.

"I'm not afraid," I told her.

"No, of course." She was still smiling, still leaning, still giving off heat like the open fireplace behind her. "Because you know that you are righteous."

"I know I've never murdered anyone."

"Because you're pure. You're strong in your convictions."

"Yes," I said. If I wasn't, I would have come over this table and done all the things to her that she was begging for. I would have been another of her men, kissing her feet and drinking her poison and happy—fucking ecstatic—to be doing it.

She reached out with one finger and tapped the rim of my cup, her fingernail stunted and almost black with dirt. "Want to know for sure?"

* * *

They split Joanie and me up almost as soon as they took us out of that cabin. It was years before she was able to ask me about that last morning, about why I ate the pancakes and never tried to purge them. "I knew I'd be okay," I said, "because Mommie gave us the dead's man's breath to send us to heaven. And I'm not going to heaven."

Across from me, Everett Priest kept his eyes on mine as he lifted the coffee cup to his lips. I didn't want him to be alone, so I raised my own cup.

It was strong and hot and sweet. One of life's little comforts.

AUTHOR'S NOTE

You can't talk about female murderers without talking about poison.

It's not exactly true that women poison more often than men (men dominate pretty much every category of murder from shooting to suffocating), but if a woman is going to kill someone, she is more likely to use poison than any other weapon, at least historically-speaking.

Poison is covert, not nearly as aggressive as strangulation or stabbing. If you aren't sure that you can physically over-power your victim, poison is a good option. Poisoning also works best when the perpetrator has some degree of intimacy with the victim and can kill them slowly, in small doses. Women's traditional role as keepers of the home, preparers of meals, and nurses for the sick meant that they were well positioned to slip a little arsenic into the meatloaf.

And that, I think, is why we really associate poison with dark femininity. Poisoning is the inverse of a woman's "natural" household role. Instead of nourishing, she destroys. Instead of healing, she sickens. Most cases of female poisoners involve members of their family and spouses.

Poisoning has come to represent the worst stereotypes of a specifically female form of evil. Poisoning is cold, patient and deceitful, dishonorable even. It is often done purely for material gain by someone who doesn't have the courage to face their victim.

It stands in stark contrast to the "hot" forms of murder associated with masculinity—crimes committed in a frenzy of anger or "passion" that are intimate and bodily and straightforward. This, too, is a kind of perversion of the traditional male role, especially when this violence is directed toward the man's family. Instead of protecting, he attacks.

Women kill because they lack feeling; men kill because of an excess of it. At least, that's the stereotype. The reality is that while many poisoners benefit materially from their crimes, that financial incentive is not enough to explain many of the more enduring cases of serial murder. There must be something more, a kind of compulsion just like the unchecked violent urges we see in more "traditional" male serial killers.

Jane Toppan, possibly the most infamous female poisoner of Victorian America (an era which boasted an alarming number of high-profile cases of murder by poison) was very frank about her reasons for murdering more than thirty people—she did it because she liked it.

Jane (born Honora Kelley) had the kind of early life that Charles Dickens would have dismissed as "too grim." Dead mother, insane father, confined to an orphanage/work house as a small child. Eventually she was indentured out as a servant.

Jane grew up curious and attracted to power. She trained as a nurse and was delighted by the opportunities this gave her to wield total control over others. She performed crude experiments on her patients, testing their reactions to non-therapeutic dosages of painkillers like morphine. She particularly liked to bring a victim as close to death as possible before reviving them and starting the process all over again. In another period, she might have been a Josef Mengele or a Shirō Ishii. Perhaps we should be thankful that the rigid gender boundaries of the time kept her from accruing too much power.

Still, Jane managed to do quite a lot of damage even as a private citizen. She poisoned husbands, lovers, landlords, even her own sister. She did not benefit financially from the vast majority of these murders and, in fact, much like her compulsive stealing, these behaviors regularly caused her to lose jobs and clients and eventually led to her arrest.

Jane Toppan couldn't help herself. She was no calculating chess master, planning out her perfect crime and then melting into the darkness. She poisoned people because that was the means she had available and because she wanted to see what happened. She even appears to have developed a paraphilia around it, often climbing into bed with her dying victims and openly stating that she derived sexual pleasure from watching them die.

The Wise Women of Nagyrév, Hungary represent perhaps a slightly more sympathetic case but, to my mind, a much more horrifying one. Nagyrév, a small, seemingly average village in Hungary, developed a murder problem shortly after World War I. Between the years of 1914 and 1929 a staggering *three hundred* people were estimated to have died poison-related deaths.

Life was hard for the women of Nagyrév. Women had little control over their lives or even their bodies. Abortion was illegal and access to even minimally effective contraception was limited. Families often arranged marriages, particularly if a girl was pregnant out of wedlock, and many a young woman found herself having a child she did not want by a man she didn't love. At this time in Hungary, marriage was a lifetime institution. Even if your husband beat you or raped you or was unfaithful to you, you were expected to remain with him until you died.

Until *one* of you died, at least.

World War I brought many of these issues to a head much in the same way that World War II raised the discussion of gender roles in America. With their men away at war, the women of Nagyrév had more freedom and autonomy than ever before. They could enter spaces previously closed to them, do work that had been forbidden, and even select lovers from the plentiful population of POWs in the village.

When the war ended, however, this new independence ended as well.

Mrs. Fazekas—the kind of "patient zero" of the Nagyrév poisonings—was what we might call a folk doctor. The extent of her medical training is unknown but in a small and rural village, she was just about the only choice for sick and injured people. She also provided abortions, which were illegal, but as they have been across time, occasionally necessary. She helped young girls get rid of unwanted pregnancies and, at some point, she took it a step further and began helping them get rid of unwanted husbands, parents, children, and whole families.

It must have been intoxicating for someone who had been shuffled from an overbearing family to a domineering, possibly even abusive, husband to suddenly have access to this incredible power—total control over their own life and the lives of others. Like Jane Toppan, the women of Nagyrév couldn't seem to stop themselves.

A heart-stopping twenty-six women were eventually tried for the killings, though likely many more had participated and still more must have tacitly condoned this long, sustained campaign of murder.

In the case of Nagyrév, the poisoners were trying to push back against restrictive gender roles, but there are some cases where murder-by-poison seems to bubble up from an overheated desire to fully embody the role of perfect mother, wife, or caretaker.

Munchausen Syndrome-by-Proxy, is a relatively new concept in the medical field and still prompts fervid debates over when and how to diagnose it. Essentially, though, a person with MSbP will deliberately sicken or injure another person to draw attention and sympathy to themselves.

This disorder is over-represented in women and most MSbP cases involve a parent victimizing a child, usually quite a young child. This is a particularly insidious form of child abuse and it has an alarmingly high mortality rate, which makes sense. Someone who suffers from MSbP is concerned above all with getting attention—from medical professionals, from strangers, even from the public at large. They need eyes on them and their child is just a tool to make that happen. Often, they don't necessarily intend to murder their victims but are also profoundly unconcerned with the physical harm they are doing to their children and incapable of stopping themselves from pushing further and further, creating ever more dire medical emergencies.

It is the strange case of Audrey Marie Hilley that I believe most fully combines all these disparate motivations. Hilley was a seemingly typical housewife, married to a modest, middle-class man with a couple of kids—and she was poisoning them. Her husband, her children, her mother-in-law, her own mother, she was feeding them all arsenic to some degree. For her husband and her stepson, it was enough to kill them. In the case of her daughter, it was a long, protracted illness that required regular medical intervention, which Hilley did not protest.

As each of them grew sicker, Hilley positioned herself as a caretaker and nurse. She also secretly took out insurance policies on them, none of the policies particularly sizable.

Arsenic poisoning is fairly well understood in the medical community, so it wasn't long before doctors recognized what was happening to Marie's last remaining child. As soon as she was discovered, Hilley bolted, leaving a somewhat confusing note suggesting that she had been kidnapped.

It gets stranger.

Hilley then met and married a man under an assumed name. During this marriage, she created a fictional backstory for herself, including an identical twin (if Hilley's story were a play, it would be called a "Chekov's Imaginary Twin"). After about a year of marriage, Hilley vanished again, offering a vague excuse about needing a medical procedure. She then proceeded to call her new husband, posing as—you guessed it—her own twin. She said that her "sister" had died and, a few months later, she returned to her husband as "Teri," her own fake twin.

This bit of unprovoked weirdness proved to be Hilley's downfall. When she tried to create a paper trail for the fake dead twin by putting an obituary in the paper, law enforcement latched on to it immediately and linked her to her original crimes.

Again, this is a case that defies the stereotype of a cool, calculating, clever serial poisoner. Everything about Hilley's actions suggests someone who was flying by the seat of their pants and regularly did things on impulse for no strategic reason.

Hilley clearly relished the caretaker role but she was also very comfortable taking lives for small amounts of money or just because it was convenient. She was erratic, impulsive, selfish, base, greedy, and not very smart.

Female killers, though they are rare, are not *special.* They aren't any more deceitful or more cowardly; they aren't smarter or less driven by profound personality disorders. They share the same attribute all serial killers have across gender, race, nation, and time—they do not value the lives of others as much as they value themselves and their desires. The packaging might be different, but the dull, dumb, ugly hearts are the same.